Blood Relatives

by

Helen Spring

Published in 2013 by FeedARead.com Publishing – Arts Council funded

Copyright © Helen Spring

The author or authors assert their moral right under the Copyright, Designs and Patents Act, 1988, to be identified as the author or authors of this work.

All Rights reserved. No part of this publication may be reproduced, copied, stored in a retrieval system, or transmitted, in any form or by any means, without the prior written consent of the copyright holder, nor be otherwise circulated in any form of binding or cover other than that in which it is published and without a similar condition being imposed on the subsequent purchaser.

A CIP catalogue record for this title is available from the British Library.

CHAPTER ONE

A hillside north of Rome - 22nd March 1944

Victoria shivered. It was a warm spring day and she was not cold, but the sight of the man trudging up the slope towards the cottage engendered a sudden frisson of fear. She pulled her thin cardigan around her shoulders, wondering if the time would ever come again when she could meet a stranger without dryness in the mouth and that instant chill. The man came on inexorably, with the heavy pushing tread of the dog tired, a toiling ant on the lazy hillside.

'Who is it?' Guiditta spoke in her usual thick southern Italian dialect, but her tone was urgent.

'I don't know.' Victoria's Italian was markedly different, flawless and without accent, the product of an expensive education and a Swiss finishing school. Understanding Guiditta's frustration she added, 'He looks harmless enough. He's young, with a pack big enough to sink a battleship.'

'No. I know Giorgio's people. I've never seen this man before.'

Victoria peered out again from behind the small lace curtain. 'He's almost here…' she said, with rising panic.

'Give me the shotgun,' Guiditta said. 'Just in case. Someone from Giorgio?' she added hopefully, 'With supplies for us?'

Victoria hesitated, but only for a moment. She crossed the room and opened a small wardrobe, moving shoes and accumulated clothes to retrieve a battered shotgun from its hiding place. She took the gun across to the truckle bed where Guiditta lay, and then scrambled to find the ammunition from the wardrobe. The old woman's lined face hardened as she took it and loaded the gun. Her thin lips pressed into a determined line as the knock came at the door.

A brief glance passed between the two women, and then Victoria went to the door and opened it. The man had taken off the heavy pack and was flexing his shoulders. He wore a tattered peasant jacket and trousers, and as he turned toward her Victoria had an impression of a wary but enquiring look, which quickly changed to a delighted smile of recognition.

'Miss Sullivan? Victoria Sullivan?' He spoke in English, with a strong American accent.

'No. I am named Vetti, Luisa Vetti.' Victoria answered in Italian, but he understood immediately and his tone changed.

'Victoria, don't give me the runaround. I've come a long way to find you. I've seen your photograph a hundred times.'

'I'm sorry, you are mistaken, I am Luisa Vetti. You have the wrong place.'

She attempted to close the door, but he pushed hard against it and in seconds was in the room, only to be brought up short by the sight of the shotgun which Guiditta leveled at his chest.

'Hey, what is this?' He was clearly taken aback and slowly raised his hands in the air. 'No need for this, ladies. I mean no harm.' Guiditta, who understood little English, made no response and he turned to Victoria. 'James wouldn't like this, you treating his buddy this way.'

'James?' She blurted it out before she could stop herself.

'Yes, James. Your brother James.' The young man's eyes flitted warily from Victoria to the shotgun. 'He is here, isn't he?'

Receiving no answer, he slowly moved his hand towards the breast pocket of his shirt, his eyes still on the shotgun. Very carefully, he unbuttoned the pocket and extracted a dog-eared photograph, which he passed to Victoria without further comment.

The shock of recognition was agonizing. Victoria sat down suddenly, as memory gnawed. She stared at the photograph of James and herself with their parents, taken shortly before she had left New York with her mother on their trip to Europe. The photograph brought with it a flood of nostalgic longings which she had thought were securely locked away.

'Where did you get this?' she whispered in English.

'From James's locker. I told you, he's my buddy.'

'Have you come from James?' Her look was desperate. 'Are the Allies in Rome at last?'

'No. We landed at Anzio in January, but we have been pinned down for months –'

'Ha!' Victoria broke in derisively. 'We know that much –'

'We're having to fight for every yard. As for James….' He stopped. 'Look, Miss Sullivan, it's important you trust me. I hoped James would be here….' He hesitated. 'Do you think you could tell the old lady to point that thing somewhere else?'

Victoria came to her senses. She spoke to Guiditta in Italian and the old woman reluctantly lowered the shotgun.

'First things first,' the man said, obviously relieved. 'Could I have something to drink?'

'We only have water,' Victoria said, but she fetched a glass from a cupboard and filled it at the water barrel in the corner. The young man dragged the big pack further into the room and took the water gratefully. He drank greedily, draining the glass, and Victoria took the opportunity to examine him in more detail. Slim build under those awful old clothes, dark hair and eyes, and a rather handsome face, she decided, perhaps a little rugged, but nevertheless.... He caught her gaze and their eyes met briefly, and she felt a quiver run through her. Not like in the romance books they used to read at school in Switzerland, no earthquake or thunderbolt, no thrill of excitement, but something ... recognition perhaps, a certain familiarity?

He did not seem to notice anything. 'Wonderful,' he said. 'Now for coffee.' He kneeled down beside the pack and began to open it. 'I've brought supplies, thought you might need them. My name is Guy by the way, Guy Waldman. You can call yourself Luisa Vetti if you want, but I know you are Victoria Sullivan.'

'You are Guy Waldman?' Victoria smiled with delight as the last of her suspicions evaporated. 'James has mentioned you many times in his letters. This is my friend, Guiditta Alvaro.'

She kneeled on the floor next to Guy as he nodded to Guiditta, and then exclaimed in delight as he emptied the pack. 'Is that sugar? Oh my Lord! It's tinned ham! Guiditta, look! Ham!' She broke off to chatter to Guiditta in Italian, only returning to English as she took a pack from Guy with an air of wonder. 'Coffee? Real coffee?'

'Yes, put the pot on, I could do with some now.' Guy seemed to have taken control of the small room and the two women. He emptied out the rest of the pack. 'There are some cans ... and these are K rations. I could eat a horse.'

As Victoria put water on the small stove to heat, she watched Guy take a trench knife from his pocket and use it to open a can of meatballs in sauce, spearing the contents and wolfing them down.

'We have knives and forks,' she said pointedly. 'And plates too, come to think of it.'

Guy stopped, a meatball halfway to his mouth.

'Sorry,' he said. 'I'm starving.'

'So are we,' said Victoria bitterly. 'We've been starving for months, waiting for the Allies to come.'

Guy stared at her. Yes, she was certainly thinner than the laughing girl in the photograph, and the old woman was staring at the meatball with a look bordering on veneration.

'And I'm waiting to know what's happened to my brother,' she continued.

Guy returned the meatball to the tin. 'OK, Pax. I'm not being difficult; I don't know where James is. That's why I came here.' He glanced at Guiditta. 'Look, I'm not supposed to say this, but I expect you already know he's in intelligence?'

'Yes, but that's all I know.' Victoria's tone was almost pleading. Guy looked away, unable to meet her eyes.

'As you know, I'm in James's squad,' he said eventually, choosing his words. 'Nearly three weeks ago he came on ahead into Rome, disguised as a local. He was to make contact with someone already here.'

'A spy, you mean.'

Guy ignored the remark. 'As I say, he came on ahead, but we've heard nothing since. He didn't make contact, and didn't return. He seems to have disappeared. James knew you were living here and told me he intended to see you if it was possible. He wanted to make sure you were alright.'

'Well, he didn't arrive.' For a moment, she felt as if she would burst into tears.

'I realize that now. At first I thought he was here, and that you were hiding him.' Watching Victoria's attempt to control her feelings, Guy added, 'Look. You make the coffee and heat up some of these meatballs for all of us, there's some more here.' He handed Victoria two more cans. 'James will be OK, you can bet on it. I've been alongside him now for more than two years, and he can take care of himself.'

As Victoria busied herself at the stove, Guy attempted to lighten the mood. 'James told me that you had a villa near Rome, left to you by your great uncle. From the line he was shooting, I thought it was a bit classier than this dump.'

Victoria smiled briefly, and beckoned him to follow her out to the small terrace at the rear of the house.

'That's my villa,' she said, pointing, a hint of pride in her voice.

'Not that...?' Guy's voice tailed away. Even from the distance of half a mile, the gracious white house across the valley was impressive.

'Yes. That's mine.'

'Wow! Then what on earth are you doing here?'

'It's been taken over by the Germans for their northern H.Q. The Oberst said I could stay, and allocated me two rooms on the top floor, but after a couple weeks I realized he wanted me to stay more for his convenience than mine.'

'I see.' He didn't, but he was beginning to.

'So I came to live with Guiditta and believe me, I was grateful to be in this "dump" as you call it. Guiditta had looked after my great uncle for many years until he died, and she stayed on with me. It was just as well I did move in with her, because a week later she fell and broke her leg.'

'So now you are looking after her?'

Victoria smiled. 'We look after each other, and we had better work out how to look after you. The Germans have lookouts with binoculars at the villa. They are on permanent watch and know every move we make. They will have seen you arrive and will certainly be here very soon.'

When the knock came at the door, they were just about prepared. The contents of the pack had been cleared away, apart from the coffee. The German soldier entered, heavy footed and glowering. The struggle up the hillside had not improved his temper.

Victoria adopted a winning smile and feigned surprise. 'Come in, Kurt. Come and have some coffee, it's just made....'

Kurt hesitated. 'You have a visitor?' His Italian was excruciating.

'Yes, come and meet him.' Victoria placed herself carefully between Guiditta and Guy, who was sitting at the low table. 'He's not bright,' she murmured. 'Doesn't hear very well, or speak much either.'

Kurt was still glowering. 'Who is he?

'He's one of Giorgio's people. He's brought us some real coffee from Giorgio. We are so lucky. I don't know how we would manage without his help.'

'Tedeschi!' said Guy, staring in amazement and apprehension.

'Have a cup with us, Kurt; it's only just been made.' Victoria ignored Guy, who cowered a little into his rough jacket. She fetched a cup and Guiditta poured coffee for the German. Victoria handed it to him and said, 'Just smell it, I'd forgotten how good it is.'

'Tedeschi!' Guy muttered again.

Victoria gave him a smile. 'Yes dear, tedeschi. He won't hurt you, will you, Kurt?' She dropped her voice. 'He gets a bit frightened when he sees a German uniform.'

Kurt took a swig from the cup. 'I've never seen him before. I thought I knew all Giorgio's people.' He drank again. 'Yes, this is good.'

'He's been with Giorgio for years, I believe,' said Victoria. 'He's called Emilio, some sort of distant relative I think-'

'Like you,' Kurt said, with a faint sneer.

'Yes, like me I suppose.' Victoria smiled but a flush suffused her cheeks. 'You won't have seen him because Giorgio doesn't use him often, for obvious reasons.'

'Tedeschi!' repeated Guy, a whimper in his voice.

'I was glad to see him though,' said Victoria, as if he had not spoken. 'He brought some cans as well.'

'Well, he'd better go before it gets dark,' Kurt said. 'It's really not safe at night for someone like him.'

'That's what I thought, and anyway he might get lost. He's going to sleep on the floor here tonight, and I'll send him back tomorrow morning.'

Kurt nodded. He finished the coffee and glanced around the small room before nodding again. 'I'll go. Can't waste time chatting, too much to do.' He walked to the door.

'I don't suppose you have any news?' Victoria asked, as if to detain him.

'About what?'

'Well, about anything. We don't have a radio and there were rumors of the Allies –'

'There are no Allies in Italy! As you say, there are just rumors, all of them rubbish!'

She opened the door and Kurt turned. 'Thank you for the coffee.'

'Oh, that's alright then,' said Victoria. 'I'll let you get on.' She closed the door and the German lumbered away.

CHAPTER TWO

After the German had gone, the tension relaxed in the small kitchen but Victoria remained tight lipped, and did not speak as she set about heating up the meatballs in sauce, and cooking the last of the pasta from the cupboard. Guy helped Guiditta to the table, and the two women enjoyed the most nutritious meal they had had for months. When it was over, Guy offered cigarettes and Victoria took one, drawing deeply as Guy lit it. Guiditta sighed and spoke sharply to her, and she turned to Guy with a smile.

'Guiditta doesn't like me to smoke, she says it is not good for me, but I haven't had a cigarette for months. I have promised her I will only smoke one.'

Guy gave an answering smile. 'Yes, I got some of what she said, but my Italian is not as good as James's, or yours.'

Victoria nodded. 'She has a very strong dialect. I've gotten used to it, but James and I both learned to speak Italian from childhood. My parents insisted on it.'

Guy lit a cigarette for himself. 'I'm afraid my Italian was picked up from the quarter where I lived in New York, with a top-up from the Army when I joined James's squad. I had Italian friends at school, and I often went to their homes for dinner.' He laughed. 'The food was better than at home.' He drew on his cigarette and then confided, 'You did well this afternoon, with the German I mean.' He smiled. 'You should join the resistance.'

'What makes you think I haven't?' Victoria smiled. 'As for Kurt, he's no problem, he's not a bad sort, just trying to do his job and hoping he'll get home in one piece, like most of us. You were lucky; a few of the others are real bastards.' She looked at Guy critically. 'I mean it, you were lucky to make it here. If your Italian is not so good, you will stick out like a sore thumb.'

Guy nodded. 'I know. I think I'll follow your idea when I go from here. Pretend I can't speak or hear properly, and act like the village idiot.'

'Even so, it's very risky. If you are caught, just remember to keep muttering "Tedeschi" as if you are afraid of them. Then perhaps they'll only beat you up. If you get arrested or taken for questioning, you could let slip the name of Giorgio, they might just let you go.'

'Who is this Giorgio?'

Victoria blushed. 'He is a distant relative; he was a friend of my great uncle who lived here before the war.'

'He wasn't in the Italian army?'

'No.' She almost laughed. 'His army is one of black marketers, thieves and smugglers. Any commodity that can be bartered, food, petrol, drink, ammunition –'

'Ah! You mean the Mafia? We have plenty of experience of them in the south … they steal our rations as fast as we land them –'

'We don't use that word, Mafia. It's an American invention. You wouldn't understand the real situation.'

'Try me.'

She shrugged. 'I'm not sure I understand it myself, probably the word we would use here is "Omerta". It means "silence", but a real silence, very deep. It does not really translate. But remember, I was brought up in New York by parents who regarded the so-called Mafia with abhorrence, as most right thinking people do.'

'But you have a connection, don't you? Your great uncle –'

'So you know?' she said bitterly. 'It's amazing how gossip can make its way across the world!'

'I only know what James told me. When we joined the Army we were buddies, and there was talk about him from the other guys, that he came from this very rich family who had links to the Mob-'

'We did NOT!' Victoria was enraged.

'I know that, calm down, will you? James told me the whole story, one night when we both had a bit to drink and were feeling sorry for ourselves. He explained it was his fault the family got that reputation, but that actually his father and mother were the best, the very best….'

'Yes, they are,' Victoria whispered. 'They truly are. They never had anything to do with the Mafia other than taking me in when my great uncle Vittorio was expelled from the States. There is no blood connection at all, but they knew my parents well. They agreed to adopt me and bring me up as their own. I was a baby, and my great uncle knew I would have a good future. He trusted them.'

'Yes, James told me. He also told me what happened to your real parents.'

Victoria sighed. 'I never knew them at all, but my mother was not anything to do with the Mob, either. Her name was Jenny, and she had the misfortune to fall in love with my father, that's all. His name was Paolo and she loved him very much. When they were killed … it was a bomb … was when I was born. The hospital could not save my mother but managed to save me. My mother – that is, my adoptive mother – always speaks of Paolo with affection, and James looked up to him like an elder brother. They were very close.'

'So you and James are not blood relatives at all?'

'No, but I feel as if we are, although he's quite a bit older than me. All my true blood relatives are here in Italy, but I was never interested in finding them until my great uncle died. I was thrilled when I found out he had left me a beautiful villa in Italy, what girl wouldn't be? Mother and I came out on a trip to Europe together. We went first to see her relatives in England, they live in the Midlands there, and then I came on here alone to see what I had inherited. Mother went back to the US. I moved into the villa and I loved it here. When the war began, at first I didn't think Italy would be affected. Then everything seemed to happen fast. I had stayed too long and I couldn't get away. It was my own fault and I've been stuck here ever since. Luckily, I have dual nationality and always spoke good Italian, so I became Luisa Vetti and was not interned.' She swallowed. 'That's enough about the past. Tell me honestly, do you think James is still alive?'

'Of course!' The response was a little too vehement. 'I can't deny it's worrying, but James is intelligent and can take care of himself.'

'But this man he was supposed to contact? He never got there?'

'No, but that doesn't mean he's been captured. Not necessarily. He may just have hit a snag and be holed up somewhere. He's wise enough to know when to keep his head down.'

Victoria nodded, but this was not of much comfort. She rose. 'Look at poor Guiditta, she's almost asleep with us rambling on and ignoring her. I'll help her to the shower and then to bed, she needs her rest.' She turned. 'When we've done, you can have a shower too, if you like. It's not much but it works.' She smiled. 'I'll see if I can find you some blankets, you'll have to sleep on that old sofa, I'm afraid. And in the morning you'll have to put those disgusting clothes back on.'

CHAPTER THREE

It's strange how the body works, Victoria pondered as she tossed in bed that night. *After the unexpected extra food, you would think I'd fall asleep easily, but I can't rid my mind of it all. After months of no news and nothing but waiting, I hear of James at last, and I've met his friend Guy Waldman.* She allowed her mind to rest gently on the image of Guy Waldman. *Not bad looking and there is something about him ... when he smiles, his face becomes alive, animated, yes, that is it. He seems full of life, full of power ... not like me, feeling so down and humiliated after being such a fool as to let myself be trapped here....* She felt she had met Guy Waldman before. *It's the eyes, when he looks at you....* She blanked out the image.

Not that there is any news really, just that James is missing and the Allies are still stuck. People go missing so easily in Rome these days ... but if he'd been captured we should surely have heard something...?

Why did I speak out like that to Guy Waldman? Almost told him my life story, not that he didn't know it already. Of course, he had no idea what was really going on. Having just arrived here with all that American openness, how could he possibly understand? Rome nowadays is not as it was when I arrived. Then, it was full of welcoming people and exciting possibilities. I was so thrilled with the beauty of it all; the architecture, the art and the countryside, the villa ... yes, most of all, my wonderful villa. Great uncle Vittorio's villa.... I wonder why he decided to leave it to me? Last time he saw me I must have been only a few weeks old.... He must have loved my father, of course, and my mother, I suppose. It would be in memory of them; that's understandable, in memory of his nephew, Paolo. Even so, I would like to have known old Vittorio. Mom always said he was not as bad as he was painted, but Dada hated him –well, I think he did. But the family was so kind to me when I first came here, you'd think they would have been mad at someone who had just inherited a lovely villa from under their noses, but they weren't, not even Giorgio. Surely he would have been expecting to inherit the villa? Yet what would we have done without his help, the bags of flour and the seeds he sent us? The pasta, and the time he sent that chicken?

Yes, times are worse now, much worse. There was worry, before, but not the underlying fear and mistrust that is with us now, since the Germans arrived. Yes, that's what it is, fear, just plain fear. Everyone has become devious, and everyone has something to hide. Sometimes it's important, if they are involved with the partisans, but often only small things, like hiding food and keeping your head down, pretending not to see things you don't wish to see, or not to know things you don't wish to know. You can't understand all this without living it, so how can I expect Guy to take it all in?

She could recall James's letter saying that Guy came from quite a poor background, at least poor when compared to their own, but he had also written, *'We get on well, he treats me as a person, not as a newspaper cutting.'* It was true, and it applied to them both. Whenever they met new people they were aware of it, the muted comments and asides. *'Isn't that the Sullivan boy who was involved in that gangland thing years ago? Isn't his sister the one with the Mafia connections?'*

It was all over long ago and had ceased to be important, but then again, when she met someone from home, someone from New York, it was the first thing they talked about; or even worse, not talked about, but studiously avoided.

Does it really matter? Now, when all I can think about is keeping alive until this hideous war is over?

The old enemy of public approbation, which had stalked her all her life in New York, which envied her wealthy lifestyle but at the same time judged that her family were "not quite the thing" seemed irrelevant in the circumstances of war, and she realized things would never be quite the same again.

If the Allies win, eventually.
If I ever get home to New York.
If James is still alive.

On the rather uncomfortable sofa, Guy had a similar problem with insomnia. Having spent three nights sleeping rough, the sofa was something of an improvement and he was dog tired, but still sleep eluded him. Despite his reassurances to Victoria, he was becoming seriously worried about James. But then he had been worried before, indeed could hardly remember a time since he joined up when James hadn't needed worrying over, or sorting out, or rescuing from some scrape or other, usually of his own making. He was a wild one sure enough, and yet Guy couldn't help liking him. James had an open and generous appetite for life which Guy envied, although it quite often got him into trouble.

Well, he might be in trouble now. Real trouble. He could have been arrested, or killed, or had an accident.... One good thing though, unlike me his Italian is perfect. I suppose that's why he was picked for this liaison work. Tomorrow I'll go back to see Rocco again, in case he's heard something....

Victoria is beautiful, he thought for the tenth time. *Obviously worried about James, and she knew who I was too. I wonder what James wrote about me? She doesn't know I've seen her before, of course, why should she? And somehow I couldn't mention it. Who would have thought that skinny little girl would have grown up to be so beautiful?*

Guy re-ran the scene in his mind, when his City College baseball team had been invited to James's home for after-game nosh. So like James, to invite not only his own team but the rival team from downtown, too. 'Mom won't mind,' he had said confidently, 'there's always plenty of food....'

There was too, and the most glamorous Mom Guy had ever met hadn't minded either, indeed, she seemed to enjoy having her huge lounge invaded by two starving baseball teams. And there was little Victoria, smiling shyly in her pink beribboned plaits, a little overwhelmed by all her brother's noisy friends but determined to be a part of it all.

The mother was beautiful, of course, he thought, *so perhaps Victoria had inherited....No, of course, couldn't be, Victoria had been adopted. Strange how James and I met again because of the Army, I recall that double-take when I met my new Lieutenant, but James remembered me right away, and was just as open and cheerful as he was in his college days. I'll bet he's been up to something and is enjoying himself no end ... and he does have a beautiful sister....*

The next morning he was aroused by the smell of coffee and found Victoria busy in the small kitchen. Guiditta was already up too, and seated in the armchair with her leg raised on a box. She winced and nodded as Guy wished her good morning, but then smiled gratefully as he found a small cushion and placed it gently underneath her foot. This time the smile was in her eyes, and Guy understood that the shotgun was no longer part of her thinking.

'Breakfast,' Victoria announced. 'We have fresh eggs courtesy of Florence, only two between us but I've scrambled them to go round, and the bread is fresh….'

'Who is Florence?' Guy was imagining a generous neighbor.

'A hen,' said Victoria, laughing. We have two, we call them Florence and Siena, but Florence is the better layer.'

'I see.'

Suddenly, the atmosphere was relaxed and cheerful. There was not much to eat, but what there was tasted good. Guy decided to open up.

'We have met once before. It was a long time ago.'

'Really?'

'Yes. At your home in New York. It was after a baseball match, James invited both teams back….'

'I remember … you were there?' She sounded quite delighted. 'Gosh, I must have been about twelve….'

He smiled. 'Do you hear much from your folks?'

Her eyes clouded. 'We write, and sometimes they are delivered. The last letter I had was several months ago, and Mom was going on and on about the war. She seems to spend her life doing parcels for our boys, and something to do with War Bonds. She seems to think she's actually involved, and asked me to write and describe what it was like here.' Victoria hesitated, and then said bitterly, 'I did, I told her it was just normal but with no food and a tiger in the backyard.' She shook her head. 'Silly really, there's no way she could understand, even if she got the letter.'

Guy nodded. 'Of course not, but perhaps that's just as well.' He hesitated. 'Look, I'm not supposed to talk about what's going on but ... did you get any leaflets?'

'Yes, last week, dropped over Rome. They were everywhere in minutes.' She got up and went over to a drawer, extracting a paper. 'Here's one.'

Guy read aloud, translating as he went: *'To the Italian people!*

As long as the Germans remain in Italy, you are condemned to destruction!

Sabotage the Germans!
Out with the Germans!

'I should have burned it, of course, but it felt like a link somehow, a link with the Allies....' She crossed the room and put the leaflet into the small stove.

'The Germans couldn't possibly stop people reading them, but they didn't need to ask. A lot of the partisans are young Communist students and don't need any urging.'

22

'How long has it been going on? Sabotage, I mean?'

'Since the surrender, I suppose, last September. That was the start of the armed resistance, at Porta San Paolo, you know it?'

Guy shook his head.

'It's a 2000 year old pyramid, near the south wall of the city. The resistance was put down ruthlessly, and the next day the Germans were in Rome.'

'I can't imagine how they could take control so easily', said Guy.

'At first they didn't seem too aggressive,' said Victoria, 'and, of course, no one knew what was happening, but they had their fifth column working in the city right away. It was all very fast. They went to all the Italian Army bureaus and at the point of a pistol disarmed the commandants, took over the offices, and sent out orders disbanding all the troops under their jurisdiction. Of course, by then they had cut all the telephone lines and were also in charge of the radio stations, and they broadcast misinformation. They posed as Italian Army officers and disarmed many Italian soldiers. Most of them had received no instructions and didn't realize what was going on.'

'Sounds pretty well-planned,' said Guy.

'No doubt of it. And, of course, this was all happening at the same time as lots of defections. General Carboni had been left in charge of the city when Badoglio left for southern Italy with the king. When he saw his boss leave, Carboni did the same, and others followed him. It all trickled down to the enlisted men, and thousands of them just left their posts and made for home, or just went AWOL.'

'What a mess….' As Guy spoke, Victoria noticed his eyes, and the way they clouded when he expressed concern. *He was easy to read,* she thought. *I wonder if he wears his heart on his sleeve?*

'A mess indeed,' she replied, 'and it still is. No one really knows what is going on. There are rumors flying around that the Germans are about to pack up and go….'

Guy shrugged. 'I've certainly seen no sign of it; we have to fight for every yard towards Rome.'

'Yes, you said.' Victoria smiled gently and for a moment it seemed she was about to say something more, something perhaps more intimate, but she simply added, 'I've packed you a few sandwiches, in case you can't find something to eat. It's some of the ham you brought us.'

'I am amazed; I thought I smelled bread baking. Don't tell me you can make bread as well!'

She laughed. 'No I can't, but Guiditta can. She got up early to do it. What I was going to say was … well … take care of yourself. I know I can't ask you what you are going to do but we'll meet again soon.'

'Yes, when the Allies come.'

Their eyes met and she felt that same quiver, but this time it was the bolt of lightning, the peculiar feeling in her stomach so beloved of the penny dreadfuls. But he only nodded, and said 'When the Allies come. I can tell you I'm going to find James, if I can. I know who he was supposed to meet, and I'll start by checking with him again, just in case James has showed up. If we do meet up, I'll find some way of letting you know he's safe.'

Her eyes brimmed with tears, but she just said, 'Thank you.'

Guy rose and put the sandwiches into his back pack. To Guiditta's surprise, he walked over to her and planted a kiss on her cheek. She tutted a little, but blushed and smiled. He held out his hand to Victoria and as their eyes met he said quietly, 'If the rumors should be right, and the Germans do leave, you must keep your heads down.'

'Do you think they will just leave?'

'No, I don't, but there may come a point when they have to, and that is when you will be in danger. I don't want to alarm you, but a retreating army often doesn't behave well. If it happens, you must hide, both of you. Anywhere you can, even if it means going up into the hills until they have gone....'

'I understand,' she said. 'We'll be careful. Good luck, and remember to act the idiot and don't speak if you don't have to.'

Guy smiled, bent slightly, and assumed the role of Emilio, shuffling his way towards the door. 'I'm just hoping the Germans' Italian is as bad as mine and they won't notice,' he said, turning towards her with a laugh. 'I have no trouble playing the idiot. Perhaps we'll meet again.'

'Yes,' she said. 'When the Allies come.'

'Yes. When the Allies come.'

After Guy had gone, Victoria and Guiditta spent a pleasant hour discussing the ways in which they could use the food Guy had brought, in order to make it last as long as possible. They still had a few vegetables they could use, although the spring crop from the small patch of garden behind the cottage was limited. Seeds had been difficult to obtain, but Guiditta had carefully hoarded some from the previous year and Giorgio had sent some. This had proved a Godsend.

It was a fine morning and Guiditta was feeling well enough to exercise her leg outdoors. Victoria joined her, and began to weed the patch under Guiditta's direction. When they had first moved to the cottage she had not had a clue about gardening. Her childhood in New York, followed by a spell in Switzerland at an expensive finishing school, had not prepared her to grow her own food. She was quick to learn, however, and found that she enjoyed it. Conversely, Guiditta had been taught to sow, nurture and harvest as a young child, and had done it all her life, and she had well-honed peasant skills learned from her father and grandfather, together with culinary secrets inherited from her mother. She joined Victoria in the vegetable patch but soon her leg began to ache, and she was forced to sit on the old garden seat and watch, while Victoria worked. Eventually, she spoke.

'The spring onions are good, we can use them soon.'

Victoria stretched. 'Yes. Can we put some more seed in?'

'Oh yes, they will grow all summer, it's the one thing we have in plenty.'

Victoria smiled and rested for a moment. She was pleased that Guiditta was looking so much better, and seemed to have cheered up with Guy's visit. She would never forget the way this old lady had welcomed her when she first arrived in Italy, how she had befriended her immediately, for no other reason than that she was the great niece of her dead employer. Of course, Guiditta had wanted to keep her place, but it was more than that. It was as if she felt that now Victoria had arrived, the long and continuous history of the villa was restored, and even if things could not return to normality, at least she could make some sort of sense of them.

Victoria regarded her friend affectionately. Guiditta had turned her face up to the sun with a rapt expression and Victoria said, 'What did you think of Guy Waldman? After you lowered the gun of course....'

Guiditta laughed. 'I was protecting us. I'll bet you couldn't have shot him if he had been a looter or a rapist.'

'I certainly could not! Anyway, what did you think of him?'

Guiditta pretended to consider. 'Oh ... I think he's ... perhaps....'

'What?'

'Good looking.' Guiditta winked.

'That's not what I meant! Really, you are hopeless; I'm going to call you Giddy.' She had to spend a moment explaining what this nick-name meant in English, and Guiditta seemed to like the idea. Then Victoria bent to the weeding, but Guiditta had already seen the deep flush suffuse her cheeks, and she smiled again to herself. What was wrong with saying Guy Waldman was good-looking anyway?

As he made his way towards the city, Guy reflected that in comparative terms, Rome had been lucky so far. His warnings to Victoria were based on his knowledge of the atrocities which had been meted out in Naples, where the Nazis had deliberately destroyed the water supply and the sewage disposal system, the electricity supply, transport and telephones, in order to bring chaos to the city and reduce the chances of organized resistance. The release of dangerous criminals from 13 prisons, looting of hospitals and kidnapping of several distinguished hostages had drawn condemnation from all quarters. Yes, Rome had been lucky so far.

It was a fine sunny morning, and Guy kept his head down and made good progress, as the few people he encountered gave him hardly a glance. When he entered the city it was siesta time, but it was quieter than he had expected. Of course, there was little petrol for cars, he thought, and Rocco had told him that bicycles were banned as well. The people he saw seemed intent on their own purposes and he quickened his pace. A part of him was amazed and delighted that he, of all people, a young American who had hardly been out of his own State, should be here in Rome, an ancient civilization which he had only heard of in school history lessons. As he gazed about him a thrill of wonder grew, and he tried to take in the beauty of the old buildings without seeming to have any interest. Soon, he was approaching the Quirinale, the palace of the absent King Vittorio Emanuele, and he reflected that for once, Intelligence had it right; the palace really did look like a wedding cake. There was a low tunnel beneath the palace, where refugees and others not wanting to attract attention gathered, and this was where James had been supposed to meet Rocco.

Guy approached slowly with his shambling gait, trying to take in the situation. A few pathetic old men were huddled together, sharing a bottle of something or other, but there was no sign of either Rocco or James. The news that there was a war on had not reached the long planted bulbs beneath the ground, and although the borders and flower beds around the palace frontage were unkempt, there was a bright flowering underneath the weeds, and in places a breakthrough of rampant colors, yellow and blue.

Guy turned, taking in the welcome sight of near normality. And then he saw him, James, on the opposite side of the road, standing on the corner smoking a cigarette. He looked as if he hadn't a care in the world, but as Guy began to shamble across the road towards him, two German officers came around the corner. They were in conversation with a youngish woman who had a dog on a lead, and the group was heading straight for James. Guy retreated to the pavement, drawing in his breath. He watched, appalled, as James smiled and intercepted them.

What on earth...? What is he doing...? The clot is actually talking to them, bending down and patting the dog ... chatting away to the young woman who is smiling and answering him. What the hell is he up to?

The Germans had moved on a little and now turned, waiting for the young woman to catch them up. This she did, turning and saying goodbye to James as she walked away. They carried on, and James returned to the corner. Guy waited a while to make sure all was clear, and then went across to him.

'James!'

For once, James looked stunned.

'What the hell, old buddy? What are you doing here?'

'Looking for you, what do you think? We've heard nothing –'

'We'd better get off the street,' James said. 'I know I'm late but I was supposed to meet Rocco here. He hasn't come.'

As they began to walk away from the palace and into the Via Raselle, Guy said, 'Rocco did come, he's been here every day for a week, it was you who didn't come.'

'Ah, well, yes, I got held up, but what the hell are you doing here?'

'I was sent to find you and report back.'

A rather dingy coffee shop was on their left. Without a word they both entered, pleased that it was almost empty. When they were seated as far from the door as possible and James had ordered, Guy repeated, in a whisper, 'I was sent to find you. The C.O. thought you were in trouble. You should have reported in a week ago.'

'I know, I know....' James was full of his rueful charm, the way he always was when he'd been misbehaving. 'O.K so I was late, but I'm here now, and who had the bright idea to send you? You can't even speak the language properly. I suppose that's why you're dressed like an old tramp?'

'It got me here anyway,' Guy said tersely. 'And what on earth were you doing talking to those Germans?'

'What Germans?'

'Those with the girl and the dog, just before I came up to you. You were talking to them.'

James looked blank for a moment, and then his face cleared. 'Oh, those Germans. I wasn't talking to them, I was talking to the dog.' He looked at Guy's stony face. 'What?'

The waiter arrived with some coffee, his grimace and shrug told them it was pretty disgusting, but the best he could do. James poured it out and looked again at Guy's closed face. 'What?' he repeated.

Guy took a mouthful of coffee and wished he hadn't. 'I don't get you,' he said, 'I don't get you at all. What the hell did you think you were doing, walking up to them like that?'

'I was looking at the dog. It was a nice dog, I like dogs. I was just asking her what breed it was, because –'

'I don't care what breed it was,' Guy snapped. 'What is wrong with you, have you forgotten we are at war and that you are a spy…?'

'I'm not a spy, not a proper one, don't be so melodramatic. I speak good Italian, there was no risk at all.'

'No risk? Where are your brains?' Guy suddenly realized he was, after all, talking to a superior officer. 'I'm sorry. I was just concerned, that's all. Anyway, where have you been? What happened?'

'Nothing really, well, nothing and everything, if you know what I mean.' James smiled and tossed back his fringe of fair hair, which had a way of flopping forward. When it became apparent that Guy was waiting for an explanation he said ruefully, 'You know me, I was happy, lying in the lee of bum island –'

'What?' Guy exploded.

'Keep your voice down!' James looked around but no one was interested. 'I had only just got here and I met this wonderful girl. Honestly Guy, if you could see her –'

'You mean to tell me you've been shacked up with some … some….'

'Careful there, she's a very nice girl.'

'I don't care how nice she is, you could get court-martialed for this!' Guy shook his head.

31

'You've pulled some stunts before but this beats all. Here we are worrying that you might be dead, and you are enjoying yourself....'

'Can't beat it,' James said, laughing. 'If I didn't know you are a po-faced bastard, I'd swear you were jealous!'

Guy sighed. 'We'll have to make up some story or other, but at least I've found you. Do you realize how worried Victoria is?'

'Victoria?' At last, James was interested.

CHAPTER FOUR

By the time Guy and James had finished their foul coffee and their subdued but antagonistic conversation, it was well into the afternoon. They left the coffee shop and made their way in the direction of Rocco's apartment, which Guy had already visited but which James had not managed to find, in spite of his mission. Guy was still annoyed that his friend, whom he admired as a role model, had behaved in such an irresponsible way. James, on the other hand, was a little crestfallen by Guy's attitude but still could not really see what all the fuss was about.

'Down here….' Guy led the way along a small narrow street. 'He's on the ground floor. We shall try the door, but if he isn't at home there is an alley alongside. We go down there and he has a small shed at the back where we can hide until he comes back.'

There was no answer to their knock, and so they made their way down the small dark alley.

'A ginnel, that's what this is,' James said. 'That's what my Mom calls them, and she's from England.'

The shed was cramped and they took some time to make themselves reasonably comfortable, moving and stacking the tools and garden chairs to make room. Guy's annoyance had cooled somewhat, and he said, 'Look, I know I went on a bit, but I can't understand how you could just play hookey when you're on a mission. Don't you care about anything at all?'

'Of course I do. I care about us all coming out of this foul war and beating Hitler, but probably not enough to kill for it, or die for it, for that matter. I care about my parents and Victoria, but all that has nothing to do with taking a few hours off to have some private life.'

'Is that what you call it? Private life?'

James bridled. 'Of course, you know all about it, don't you? You think I was just playing around with some tart.' He stopped. 'Why should I try to explain? You've already made your mind up.'

'How can I have made my mind up about anything when I'm completely in the dark?'

There was silence for a few moments and then James said sullenly, 'You have made your mind up that whoever and whatever she is, I shouldn't have been with her. And that anything we have together is not serious –'

'How can it be serious? You must have only known her for five minutes!' Guy felt himself growing angry again. 'And you are right on one point, you should have been attending to your job....' He stopped. 'I'm sorry, I shouldn't have said that.'

Silence descended again, but James had the grace to respond. 'No, you shouldn't, but I know you are only trying to look out for me. You're right, I have been irresponsible, but once in a while something happens to you that you can't ignore, something you just have to pick up and run with, whatever the cost or the problems. Something so wonderful that you just can't deny it or....' His face had become energized, his tone urgent, as if pleading to be understood.

'That good?' Guy couldn't help but smile. 'Tell me about it.'

'Well,' James said sheepishly, 'I met her when I was picked up by the first contact when I arrived, a guy called Julio, he was very helpful and took me to his home. While I was there she called to see him. She is his sister, she is called … Chiara.' He said the name softly, savoring it, and when he looked up his eyes were ablaze.

'She's wonderful, Guy. She's absolutely the most wonderful person….'

Guy laughed. 'I get the picture.'

'I'm sure you don't,' James said, smiling. 'You can't possibly imagine … it's not that she is so beautiful, although she is. She speaks excellent English so we can communicate really well, and it's as if I've known her forever. It's just that there is something there … something so special … it was there the moment we met, and the greatest thing of all is that she feels it too.'

'True love, then?' Guy was only half joking.

'O.K, O.K, I know how it sounds –'

James stopped mid-sentence, as without warning a huge explosion reverberated around them. It was so loud that the little shed rattled and some of the tools fell over. For a moment, Guy thought they were under attack.

'God! What was that?' James whispered, his hand to his mouth.

'A bomb … that's what that was.' Guy was equally shocked. 'It had to be a bomb, but I didn't hear a plane….'

Three shattering blasts in quick succession had them both on their knees, arms over their heads. They remained crouched for a few minutes, and then Guy said, 'I'll just go along the alley and see if I can see anything.'

'I don't think that's a good idea,' said James, as they slowly got up and peered out of the shed window. 'Something big has happened.'

Guy was already halfway out of the door. 'I'm not going far.'

As he made his way down the small back garden and along the alley, he could hear sporadic gunfire. When he reached the road and looked back the way they had come, he saw a dense cloud of smoke rising over the whole quarter. He hurried back to the shed.

'It seems like some sort of explosion, must be huge judging by the smoke. Something big is afoot, no doubt about it. We can't risk moving. The best thing to do is stick to the plan and wait here for Rocco.'

James nodded. The air and the mood had turned sour. They stared at each other grimly, and then settled down to wait.

Victoria had a sense of relief as she made her way down the gentle slope at the back of the cottage. It was good to get away, even for a short while, and the afternoon was warm and clear. From the edge of the field bordering the cottage garden, she could see far along the valley, to where scattered buildings indicated the outskirts of the nearest town. The valley was mainly rich farmland, or at least it had been until the populace had been diverted to other activities, the all demanding activities of war. Now they were soldiers, or prisoners, or working in factories or.... 'Heaven knows what,' Victoria muttered, regarding the unkempt grasslands. Even the cattle seemed to have deserted, sold long ago with no one left to ensure the age-old continuity which had been so reliable, so taken for granted.

'Bloody war....' she swore as she climbed over the fence and began to scour the field. Last year there had been mushrooms, quite a few of them, and Guiditta had said it was worth looking, although they were not as easy to spot now the grass was so long.

After ten minutes searching without result, she sat down and relaxed, enjoying the sun's warmth and the peace of the place. This was still a beautiful spot, she thought, despite the war and all that came with it. In a way it was better than being in the city, where everything was becoming dilapidated and worn down, including the people. Here at least there was fresh air and a little solitude from time to time, where she could escape inside her head and be with her family in New York. She felt a little guilty about what she had said to Guy about her mother. Something about her thinking she was doing something because she was buying War Bonds and sending out parcels. That was unfair; after all, what else could she do? She was doing what she could, like everyone else, and when Victoria thought about it, receiving one of those parcels would be very welcome indeed. Despite all the news about fighting and dying and planes and ships and armies on the move, there were other ways of helping. She was aware she hadn't done much lately, not since the time when she had been recruited to join the army of volunteers who had filled out hundreds of thousands of fake census returns. She could hardly stop from laughing out loud even now, as she remembered it. That would teach the Germans to think they could count and categorize the Roman population! Simply by word of mouth the message had reached everyone, non-cooperation. Everyone filled in their census form, but with fictitious names and addresses, or sometimes real ones from the other side of the city, and some particularly keen citizens even swapped houses and apartments with relatives and friends for a few weeks, just to confuse things. The Italian partisans and Trade Unions had printed up over a million extra forms, and teams of volunteers had filled them out and mailed them to the Census bureau. After a few days of trying to check this mythical population, the Germans, drowning in a sea of paper, had given up and thrown away all the nonsensical data.

Victoria smiled again and chewed on a piece of grass. It had been fun to be involved, but since that time she had hardly been into Rome. Apart from the difficulty of getting there, with the filo-bus running so erratically and often stopped by German patrols, it was not pleasant to be in Rome at the moment. Over the months it had become ever more dangerous, a city of spies, double agents, informers, escaped prisoners, hunted Jews and hungry people. Many still clung to the idea that because Rome was the Holy City, it would be protected from the worst excesses that the Germans had inflicted on other cities. Victoria was not so sure about this. She recalled what Guy had said about armies in retreat. If the rumors about the Allies were true, it would perhaps not be long before the Germans began to move out. She could hardly bear to think about it, because the idea of being able to move back into her own lovely villa with Guiditta was a dream she had resisted for so long. She had closed her mind to the possibility because it had taken all her time and effort just to keep herself and Guiditta alive. But perhaps … perhaps…. But that was when Guy had said they would be most vulnerable.

She scanned the landscape, there did not seem to be any obvious hiding places. Suddenly it came to her ... there was a small cave they had found one day, when they had been picnicking. They had stopped below a big rocky outcrop to take advantage of the shade, and Guiditta had said, 'If you want real shade you could go into the cave, it's just round there...' pointing a little further along the outcrop. The entrance had been hardly visible, and she had just taken a quick look, but it occurred to her now that it might indeed be a good place to hide if it ever became necessary. She decided to investigate and refresh her memory, and when she returned to the cottage almost an hour later, she indulged in the thought that Guy would have been pleased with her afternoon's work. Guy ... she allowed her mind to dwell on his face; that look in his dark eyes when he had promised, 'When the Allies come.' How long would it be before she would see him again? Before the war ended? At home in New York? He had not said exactly where he lived.... She climbed back over the fence into the cottage garden. Guiditta would be pleased, she had found three mushrooms.

CHAPTER FIVE

It was almost three hours before James and Guy saw any movement. They were uncomfortable and hungry, and James at least was certain that Rocco wasn't coming.

'Perhaps he was involved in it, whatever it was,' he had said more than once. 'Perhaps he's been picked up by the Boche. If he has we need to move, before they come to turn his place over….'

'If that had happened, they would have been here already', Guy said firmly. 'And if he was involved, or even anywhere near it, he will be lying low until it's safe to move. Rocco knows what he's doing.' He only hoped his confidence was not misplaced. He had only met Rocco once, and if he had been arrested they would both be vulnerable.

'There!' Guy spoke tersely. 'There he is!' They watched as the stocky man, dressed in working clothes and carrying a bag, came along the alley and stopped at the back door. He glanced behind him anxiously and then inserted a key in the door and quickly went in.

'We'll give him a couple minutes,' said Guy, 'and then we'll go in.'

They moved quietly to the back door and James knocked lightly. They received no answer so he knocked again, but still very quietly. The door opened an inch.

'Who is it?' The voice was low and nervous.

'I was told you might have vegetables for sale.' James used the code he had been given, and spoke in Italian.

'It's a bit early for spring greens,' came the reply.

James replied quickly, 'Onions will do.'

The door opened.

Rocco stared at them and then took Guy's hand. 'I was hoping you were OK,' he said. His Italian was heavily accented. He stared at James. 'Is this him?' His tone was none too friendly.

James put out his hand. 'Yes, I'm Wilson,' he said, using his code name. 'Sorry I was held up.'

Rocco ignored the hand. 'Do you know how long I'm waiting for you to show up? An hour every day for four days! It was miracle I'm not seen!'

'Yes, I'm sorry,' James replied. 'I was held up —'

'Not easy coming through the lines,' said Guy. 'But what's been happening? We were hiding in the shed and heard the most God-awful noise, sounded like an explosion.'

'Come through.' Rocco led the way into a small kitchen. He lit an old fashioned oil lamp, and motioned them to sit down at the table. He was obviously upset. 'Yes,' he said at last, 'it is an explosion. Someone - partisans - detonated a bomb just as a column of German soldiers is marching through Via Rasella. It is chaos - terrible!'

'Were they successful?' James asked eagerly.

Rocco stared at him. 'If you mean they kill German soldiers, yes, at least twenty-five - perhaps more - and others injured. Do you call it successful? I hardly know … it depends what they do now….'

'We heard some shooting afterwards.'

'Yes.' Rocco nodded. He still looked shaken. 'Some Germans start firing at hotel windows and other places but no one was firing back. They were in panic. It was stopped by one of the officers. People were running everywhere. Then the Germans who were OK were arresting anybody they could catch, anyone at all. Chaos … just chaos…. There were lumps of concrete flying and a great hole in a wall and water gushing through….'

'Where were you?' asked Guy.

'I was at the bottom of the road, near the end of the column. There must have been around a hundred and fifty, they march through there every day, I've seen them often enough. They always have escort at the front, about six with submachine guns, and an armored truck at the back with machine gun, you know, mounted on platform. As soon as the explosion happens, I run into one of the shops and out of the back. All I can see is chaos. Chaos!' Rocco's lined face creased further at the memory. 'There was so much blood everywhere, many soldiers dead and many wounded and screaming. People running everywhere and all the dust and some soldiers shooting just anything at all….' He shook his head angrily. 'I am lucky to get away; the Germans were picking up everyone, shopkeepers, and the customers, anyone who happens to be there. I was not daring show my face until now. They are still looking for partisans, but where are they? Gone long ago, I think.'

'It sounds well planned,' said James. 'Do you know who did it?'

Rocco turned away. He made a dismissive sound, as if he did not think much of whoever it was.

'Tch!' It was almost a sneer. 'I do not know for sure, but there are several groups who have more bravado than sense.' Seeing James's raised eyebrows he said fiercely, 'Do not misunderstand, Wilson. I rejoice - yes! I rejoice that we killed Germans! And those who did this planned it well, you are right about that. But what have they left behind? What will happen now to all those people the Germans have taken? I was told there were at least two hundred herded together against the big gates outside Palazzo Barberini.'

'But –'

'You do not understand, Wilson! You do not know what the Germans will do.'

'And neither do you, Rocco.' Guy's tone was quiet, conciliatory. 'You are right, we now have a tense situation here, and so we must be even more careful. We have to report back to HQ about the situation here, and get back to our lines as soon as we can. It will be more difficult now, both for us and for you and your friends.'

Rocco did not answer, but he got up and filled a saucepan with water and put it on the small stove. 'I'll make coffee,' he said, and then added, 'Coffee! What I mean is, we use these grounds – again.' He opened the top of the coffee pot and sniffed it suspiciously. 'Should be OK, just once more.'

Guy and James exchanged a glance, and Guy shook his head, mouthing, 'Victoria – I gave it to her.' James nodded.

'I have just a little more to do here in Rome,' he said. 'Is it alright for us to stay here for a couple more days?'

'No!' Rocco was vehement. 'This trouble has changed everything. We are much too near the explosion. The Germans will be raiding every house in the area; it is what they always do if they are threatened. You must go right away! Well, as soon as it gets dark.'

'Where?' James asked.

'You can go to Julio, don't worry, you will be safe there. Do you have to stay as well?' he asked, turning to Guy.

'No,' James answered for him. 'Guy will go back to our lines and let them know I'm OK and on my way. No point in both of us taking more risks.'

Guy raised his eyebrows a little at that, but as Rocco turned to make the so-called coffee, he whispered, 'What do you have to do?'

'Only a little more reconnaissance – I know you think I've done nothing since I've been here, but I did in fact do most of it with Julio's help before I even met Chiara. He knew all the main sites the Germans are using. You can tell me what you know about their northern HQ. I know they took over Victoria's villa and you have been there, I need as much information as possible. There must be a plan for the retreat, the German brass know it is inevitable by now. It would be helpful to know exactly how they plan to leave.'

'What? You must be joking. I don't think they imagine it's inevitable at all. When I came through the lines it was plain they were dug in for the duration. We are going to have to fight towards Rome, yard by yard.' Guy leaned forward as Rocco came to the table with mugs of dirty brown water. He had caught the end of the conversation and said, 'So you think the Allies are not coming?'

'We are coming,' James said firmly. 'We are here, and we are coming to Rome. Just not as soon as you would like.'

'If you take much longer there will be nothing to take,' Rocco answered. 'Rome is near starvation, you do not understand how things are. A great city with a famine is a hard place to be.'

'I know,' said James, 'but we are not coming here to "take" anything. It is not General Alexander's orders to occupy Rome. Only to drive through, to drive the Germans out before us and pursue them all the way back home.'

'There was a riot yesterday,' Rocco said, as if James had not spoken. 'At a baker's shop, people complaining he was putting too much sawdust in the bread. They wanted to lynch him because when they managed to get a loaf, they couldn't chew it. I was sorry for the poor bastard. He couldn't do anything else because he didn't have any flour. He had been trying to stretch it out as long as possible to produce something, no matter how bad. Now he is closed, like the others.'

Guy realized they were not going to get anything to eat. 'Perhaps you can give us directions to Julio's house,' he said. 'We'll be out of your hair as soon as we can.'

Rocco nodded. 'I shall take you first part of the way.'

CHAPTER SIX

When the summons came next day, Victoria was in the small back garden hanging out some washing. Guiditta appeared at the kitchen doorway, she looked disheveled and a little panicky.

'Luisa,' she said urgently. 'Kurt is here, you have to go to the villa.'

Victoria was immediately on her guard. Guiditta only called her "Luisa" when she was trying to warn her. Victoria had not been lying when she insisted to Guy that her name was Luisa Vetti. It was the name she had used since the occupation. Vetti had been her great uncle's name, and was well known in the area. The German military accepted it readily enough.

The reason for caution was plain. Kurt appeared behind Guiditta, peering out.

'Come quick, Oberst Fleischer want you.'

There it was –the fluttering of the heart, the constriction of the throat so that even if she tried to swallow her fear it was like swallowing a stone. Why did he want to see her? Their last meeting, when she had informed him she was leaving the villa to take up residence in the cottage, had not been friendly. Victoria could not imagine what he wanted now. That had been three months ago, surely he was not about to make another pass? Or to punish her for her rejection of what he saw as a generous offer?

As she quickly dried her hands and picked up her cardigan, she attempted to make her tone light. 'What does he want? Do you know?'

Kurt just shrugged and lumbered away down the path, turning and gesturing for her to hurry. She met Guiditta's fearful eyes and smiled. 'Don't worry, it will be alright. It won't be anything much....'

Guiditta nodded, but as she watched Victoria hurry away after Kurt she crossed herself and offered up a muttered prayer.

Although part of her wanted desperately to see what had happened to the villa during the recent months, Victoria kept her gaze averted as she was led through the big entrance hall towards Oberst Fleischer's study. It would only arouse suspicion if she showed too much interest. Kurt knocked on the heavy oak door and then opened it, motioning her through.

The room was as she remembered it, a large square room with an extensive bay window overlooking the garden. Oberst Fleischer was standing in the window with his back to her, hands behind his back, looking out. He did not turn as she entered, and Victoria had time to quickly observe that all seemed to be in order. Her great uncle's big desk was now in the center of the room, having been moved from its original place against the wall, when the room had served as the main living area of the house. She allowed her gaze to wander around the lovely cornices and the large fireplace, which now held no fire but had two large filing cabinets dominating the hearth. She waited, nervously, but when the Oberst eventually turned, he looked mildly surprised to see her.

'Ah yes ... Miss Vetti ... how are you?'

His English was slow but correct, and Victoria remembered he had told her he had spent two years studying in England before the war. He had always spoken to her in English, as his Italian was poor. His question did not seem to require an answer, so she smiled slightly and nodded in acknowledgement.

'Do take a seat....' He indicated the chair on her side of the desk and sat down, regarding her with remote and cold scrutiny. It was a look which made her imagine a big cat, which outwardly seemed pleasant and docile, but which was making up its mind whether or not to eat you.

Oberst Fleischer was probably in his late forties, and his well pressed uniform and upright bearing made him look every inch the military man. Of average height and build, his face, while not exactly good looking, had a regularity of features which was quite pleasing, and his light brown hair grew thickly, although peppered with strands of grey. His eyebrows, which now gathered together in a slight frown, were well shaped and as Victoria met his gaze she flinched, because the eyes were pale blue and cold, and held a look of disdain –even menace. She felt chilled and revolted by his intense scrutiny, and tried to gather her wits. The narrow lips however formed a polite smile as he said, 'Thank you for coming.'

As if I had a choice, Victoria thought, but she smiled again and waited. Whatever he wanted to say he was a long time about it.

'How do you manage in that old cottage?' The tone was light, but not really interested.

'Very well thank you. Well, we could do with more food, but otherwise we are OK.'

He considered this and then remarked, 'It was not my doing that you are there. You could have still been here, on the top floor. I did offer you that.'

What the hell is this about? 'Yes, of course.'

'Then why did you leave?' The sharp rejoinder hung in the air.

You know why I left, you bloody pervert, because I wouldn't go along with your plans for me.... She blushed slightly as she said, 'Well, it was for Guiditta really. I wanted to take care of her, as you know she has broken her leg, and she couldn't have made the top floor....'

His face visibly relaxed, and Victoria went on, 'I don't know if you are aware, but she was housekeeper to my great uncle for many years, so of course I feel a responsibility.' *And if you believe that, you'll believe anything. We both know why I went. Guiditta didn't even break her leg until after we moved in to the cottage.*

'Of course, I understand.' He seemed to find nothing strange in her explanation and came to a decision. 'In that case, Miss Vetti, perhaps you will be good enough to sign this document.' He opened the top drawer of his desk and extracted a piece of paper. 'It is a statement to say that when your house was occupied by ourselves, we behaved in an exemplary manner, both to you as the owner, and to the house itself.'

What is this you bastard ... what are you up to? She said, apologetically, 'I don't quite understand...?'

'It is just an acknowledgment, that is all ... that as the occupying force we have carried out our duties correctly....' He leaned forward. 'Well, we have, haven't we? We have not damaged the place in any way....'

'No, of course you haven't,' she agreed with a smile. *I see! Yes, of course! You think the Allies are coming ... you're afraid you are going to lose and you're covering your back....* A great sense of triumph swept through her. *It must be! The Allies are on their way and he knows it!*

Quietly she said, 'I don't quite see –'

'And in return,' Fleischer interrupted, 'I shall give you a letter detailing the facts of our occupation of the property, and you will be able to claim reparation from the German government ... rent ... you see?' He paused, and then said, 'It is standard procedure for the German army.'

'Oh, I see, yes of course.' Victoria took the pen he offered and signed her name, Luisa Vetti, and Fleischer took it back and signed another prepared document which he handed to her. Victoria glanced at it, and discovered the German government owed her a great deal of money. *Some hopes!*

'Does this mean, Herr Oberst, that you may be leaving soon?' She spoke with an innocent smile.

His face was closed. 'Of course not, but it is possible there may be ... we never know when our orders are going to change, and I like to have things up to date....'

He rose. The interview was over. As Victoria left the room she turned and saw he was once more standing in front of the window. As if he felt her look he said, 'Auf Wiedersehen, Miss Vetti.'

'Goodbye, Herr Oberst.'

As she left the room she could almost swear she heard him gritting his teeth.

Guiditta was waiting anxiously when Victoria returned to the cottage. 'What is it?' she asked right away. 'What is happening?'

'I don't really know.' Victoria sank onto the old sofa where Guy had slept, and relaxed. 'He wanted me to sign a document saying that they had behaved properly, you know ... not done any damage... and he gave me this.' She took a paper from her jacket pocket and handed it to Guiditta, who glanced at it in disgust.

'It's in German!' she protested. 'What does it say?'

'It says the German Army owes us rent. There, at the bottom, that's how much they owe us.'

'What?' Guiditta's face was a picture. 'Will they pay it?'

Victoria smiled. 'I very much doubt it, what do you think?'

'I think they are getting nervous.' Guiditta became animated. 'Why else would they do this now? They never mentioned anything about rent before, did they?'

'Not a word.'

'Well, now they are getting worried. They are afraid the Allies will come and they will be taken prisoner, and they want to look in a good light, and pretend they were never the evil bastards we know they are.' Guiditta scowled, the lines on her face deepening as she made a dismissive movement. 'I knew! I knew when your friend Guy came, the Allies are nearer than we thought.'

'I agree. But I'm not sure about the Germans being taken prisoner. They may make the decision to fight for Rome until the last man, but if they don't, I think they will just run for it.'

Silence fell as both women considered this. Then Victoria said, 'Do you remember what Guy said about armies in retreat? He said they don't behave well. If the German army does retreat, it will come this way. We know the Allies are pushing from the South.'

'Not officially, we don't. We don't know anything, only what we have heard via Giorgio, and that isn't necessarily true.'

Victoria nodded. 'I know, but it seems logical, and we have to plan on that assumption –'

'Plan? What plan? Victoria, what do you have in mind?'

'Saving our skins, Guiditta, that is what I have in mind, and the sooner we get ourselves organized, the better.'

By the time Guy and James reached the northern outskirts of the city, they were both exhausted and ravenously hungry. Rocco had insisted on accompanying them for at least three miles, until he led them towards some abandoned farm buildings.

'We shall rest here,' he said. 'Just ten minutes.'

They followed him wearily, but once inside Rocco switched on his torch and led them to a corner. He pulled back a worn tarpaulin to reveal two old bicycles.

'Good,' said Rocco. 'I was not sure they would be here. They have been left for you by some friends … macchia.'

James smiled with relief. 'God bless the Resistance!'

'Be careful,' Rocco ordered. 'They are old and God knows how long they will last. The brakes may not work.'

'Never mind that,' Guy said. 'They'll do.'

'Also to remember,' Rocco said firmly, 'bicycles are forbidden since December. If you are seen you will be arrested, so no lights.' He did not explain how they could find their way in the dark. He turned. 'I will say goodbye to you now. You will go ahead along this lane for about four miles, until you see a small shrine on the left. It is white with a statue of Our Lady.' Rocco crossed himself, and continued, 'If there are fresh flowers placed there it is safe to go on. You turn left and follow the track to the farmhouse; they will take care of you there.'

'What if there are no flowers?' asked James.

Rocco shrugged. 'Then I don't know … you must do your best.' He led the way out of the barn, and Guy got the distinct impression he was glad to be rid of them.

'Thank you, Rocco,' James whispered. 'We'll see you in Rome, when this thing is over. I'll buy you a drink.'

Rocco nodded, but as he slowly walked away he did not turn back. Guy said quietly, 'Poor bastard, he's got to walk all the way back home now.'

By the time they reached the small white shrine the bicycles did not seem so much of a blessing. They were both old and rusty, Guy's brakes did not work, and James's chain came off twice. Nevertheless, they were heartened to see the small bunch of wild flowers which adorned the base of the statue, and made their way carefully down the rough track, which was even more potholed than the lane. It was very dark and almost impossible to see where they were going, but the evening air was soft and warm and after a few hundred yards James stopped, entranced by the sight of a small swarm of fireflies, which danced and glowed in the hedgerow.

'Look, Guy,' he whispered, as Guy's bike narrowly missed a collision. 'Look.'

'What is it?' Guy peered.

'Fireflies … did you ever see anything so lovely? They've come out to light our way!'

'Well, I hope they light the way to the farmhouse,' Guy retorted. 'For God's sake stop playing the nancy-boy and get a move on.'

'OK, OK.' James got back on his bike and pedaled away, and they had only gone about fifty very bumpy yards when a dark figure suddenly emerged in front of them.

'Who goes there?' It was a low voice, speaking Italian.

'Oh! It's us….' James was nonplussed for a moment. 'I mean … I was told you might have vegetables for sale.'

'It's a bit early for spring greens,' came the reply.

'Onions will do,' James responded, and the figure waved them to follow him.

CHAPTER SEVEN

It was difficult to gain any real impression of the building as Guy and James approached it. The darkness was intense, and they pushed their bicycles hesitantly as they concentrated on the shadowy form of the man leading the way. All they could see was a rather bulky outline in dark clothing, with an occasional glimpse of a beckoning hand when he turned to encourage them on. When he stopped and indicated they should leave the bicycles against a low wall, it took a moment to realize they were within a few feet of a building with a large door. The ancient iron hinges made James suspect a medieval castle rather than anything else. There was no time to find out however, because the door opened and for the few seconds it took to pass inside, there was a momentary shaft of light. They found themselves in a gloomy hallway of stone walls and floor, and were then led to an adjacent room, hearing the buzz of voices as they approached.

As they entered the room fell silent, and they were subjected to avid scrutiny from the four people arranged around a long wooden table, which bore the remains of a meal –or at least, the empty plates. There were three men and one woman, and as soon as they entered, James blurted out, 'Chiara.' Although the woman did not respond, Guy saw her give a sideways look of recognition at James as she turned away, and suddenly Guy understood how James had become so involved. The woman was very beautiful and it was obvious there was something between them.

The man who had met them took it upon himself to make the introductions, and addressed the gathering. 'These are the American friends we were expecting.' Turning towards James, he said, 'My name is Carlo, and we have here Federico, Emilio and Giuseppe. I think you know Chiara already.'

The three men nodded. Federico pushed back his chair and picked up a piece of wood, which he proceeded to whittle with a sharp knife. He was middle aged and needed a shave and a haircut, and his clothes looked as if they had been slept in for weeks. Emilio, on the other hand, was young and possessed of those Italian good looks so evident on the streets of Rome. James mentally filed him as a city boy, and wondered briefly why he was not in uniform. Giuseppe was the eldest of the three. He wore a grizzled beard and a sour expression, and James decided he would not care to cross him. James and Guy stepped forward and offered handshakes, which were taken reluctantly, except for Chiara, who smiled delightedly and said quickly, 'Have you eaten? There is not much but I can find you some soup....'

'That would be great,' said James, turning to translate for Guy, who had understood but nodded his thanks. Carlo indicated they should sit down at the table, and instructed Emilio to move the bicycles. Emilio shot them a look of cool dislike, but got up and went out.

'We could have moved the bicycles ourselves,' said James with a smile. He did not receive one in return. Giuseppe said shortly, 'If you go out and get caught, we are all dead. If Emilio gets caught, he can talk himself out of it.'

James saw the look of apprehension on Guy's face and did not reply. They were in uncharted territory here, and he was aware he could easily put his foot in it.

An uncomfortable few minutes passed until Giuseppe spoke again. His English was rough and matched his manner. 'Did you see it? Were you there?'

For a few moments James did not understand, but then he said, 'You mean the attack in the Via Rasella? No, we weren't there, but we were only a couple streets away. We only know what Rocco told us, there were quite a few Germans killed and wounded –'

'Ha!' The sound was dismissive.

'You don't sound impressed,' James said. 'I suppose like Rocco, you think this attack might have been a mistake?'

'There is no knowing,' Giuseppe responded shortly.

Chiara came back to the table with two bowls of vegetable soup and some bread. She smiled at James. 'The bread is hardly edible, but it's OK if you dip it in the soup and swallow it quickly.'

'It's fine,' James responded. 'You can't imagine how hungry we are....'

He stopped, realizing that since the invasion the food shortage had meant everyone there understood exactly what it was like to be really hungry. 'Sorry', he said, dipping the bread. 'This is wonderful.'

Carlo came across and sat next to Guy as Emilio rejoined them. Carlo leaned across the table to James. 'If the Allies were on the doorstep it would be different. Then we would be doing all we could to disrupt the Germans in whatever way we could. But now … we have nothing to fight them with. Many innocent people have been taken and there is no news of what has happened to them, we have no way of helping them. If we knew the Allies were here tomorrow, we could take risks, but we have been waiting so long….'

Giuseppe got up and strode to the door. 'I'm going to bed. No more talk. Too much talk.' He went out.

Carlo shook his head. 'Don't mind Giuseppe. He has already lost a son and he is frustrated at the lack of action while we wait for the Allies.' He stretched out his big frame and yawned. 'We should all make an early night. Tomorrow, Julio should be back, he has contact with your lines, and we hope to have some news for you.'

It was early afternoon the next day before Julio finally arrived. By that time, James and Guy had familiarized themselves with the layout of the building, which in daylight proved to be nothing more sinister than a solid old farmhouse, surrounded by fields long stripped of any crops.

Guy found himself eager to meet the legendary Julio, because when at last they were lying in the narrow beds assigned to them the previous night, James had explained to him that Julio was Chiara's brother, and was in charge of this group. James had spent some time with him when he first arrived in Rome, and rated him highly for his knowledge and commitment. As introductions were hastily made, and they took their places around the kitchen table, Julio seemed more interested in what had happened in Rome than anything else. He said there were plenty of rumors but not much official information, or even underground information, which could be relied upon.

'It seems the only thing we really know is that the Germans have taken many hostages and are holding on to them,' he said. 'Heaven knows what will happen next. We are trying to find out just who is being held and why, but the Germans are answering no questions. All we have to go on are reports from relatives of people who are missing, and there seems to be nearly three hundred of them so far.'

Julio stretched his arms. It was obvious that he was weary from his overnight travel and was anxious for bed. Looking at him, the likeness to Chiara was apparent; the dark eyes with long lashes and the slightly patrician features. Two very good looking people, Guy thought, wondering about their childhood together. They seemed to be quite close in age, and he speculated for a moment that they could be twins.

'So many hostages?' James queried. 'The number seems to be growing by the minute.'

'That's what I mean,' Julio said. 'The figures are so unreliable. Anyway, to business, although it may not be to your liking.'

James and Guy leaned across the table towards him as he lowered his voice.

'I have your orders, James,' he said, taking an oilskin wrap from his breast pocket and handing it over. 'It means you go back to Rome.'

'Oh … OK.' James began to unwrap the small package.

'What about me?' Guy queried, and Julio shrugged his shoulders.

'That is up to your officer here.' Like Chiara, he had very good English. He rose stiffly. 'I'm off to bed, unless there is anything else I can do for you?'

James was reading the orders. 'Only one thing,' he said. 'Are you my only contact?'

Julio hesitated. 'As far as contacting your HQ is concerned, yes. But if you have any difficulties in Rome, you could contact a local guy called Giorgio. He's a bit of an unknown character, local big man, but he has cooperated and knows your sister, the one with the villa.'

'Yes, I've heard of him,' Guy said. 'He's Mafia, isn't he?'

Julio glowered. 'Amici, yes. You have to make choices. At least he's not a *fascista*. He won't sell you out to the Germans.' He lumbered to the door. 'If I don't see you again, good luck.'

Guy watched expectantly as James read the orders. He took his time, and then said, 'Well, would you believe it; we have to contact Victoria again. It seems we have to gain access to the German Northern HQ.'

'You mean to Victoria's villa?'

'Precisely. They need us to find out the German deployments, and plans for the retreat.'

'Retreat? They probably don't have any. They don't look like they're intending to retreat anywhere –'

'Perhaps not just yet, but they will have a plan, and there will be orders in place to be carried out once a retreat is decided on.'

'If it's decided on,' said Guy. 'It looks to me like they're intent on fighting all the way.'

'Even so,' countered James calmly. 'General Clark will need to know how many divisions are needed to drive on to Rome, and how many to follow up the retreat … depending on which way they go.'

'You seem very sure they'll go,' Guy grumbled. 'What about me?'

'Well, I'll need you to get me there.' James laughed. 'By a stroke of luck, you've already been there and know the way.'

Guy felt a small thrill of pleasure. He was going to see Victoria again. 'It wasn't luck at all,' he said. 'It was strategic planning.'

As Victoria climbed her way through the lower field and back to the cottage, she felt a small glow of satisfaction. This was her fourth visit to the cave and already she had managed to secrete enough food and equipment to ensure that she and Guiditta could hide out there if needed, for a few days anyway.

Guiditta was sitting near the vegetable patch in the sun. She motioned Victoria to come and sit on the low wall beside her. 'Come and rest,' she said, 'you will be exhausted if you go on like this.'

'I'm OK,' Victoria smiled. 'It's all going quite well. Now we have somewhere to go if things get tricky.'

Guiditta nodded. They sat in the sun, letting the warmth seep into their bones.

'You know,' Victoria said, 'on a morning like this I can start to believe that it will happen, that one day the Boche will be gone and we shall be able to make plans for the future. We have to think what we are going to do with the villa, long term, after all this is over.'

'Yes.'

'Well, what do you think?'

'Yes....' Guiditta stopped, and then started again. 'I should tell you something.'

'What is it?'

She frowned. 'It might not be good to know this … but if it gets tricky … what you call tricky….' She seemed to like the word.

'What is it? Just spit it out.'

Guiditta sighed. 'If you don't want to know, we can pretend I didn't tell you –'

'For goodness sake!'

Guiditta looked apprehensive. Then, 'There are guns.' She said it quietly.

'Guns? What guns? Where?'

'In the attic. In the attic in the villa.'

'How do you know?'

'I put them there.' Guiditta's voice was low, as if she did not want to be heard, although there was no one else there.

'Tell me.'

'When your great uncle died, there were several guns which he kept at the villa. A couple shotguns for hunting, and a rifle and three different handguns, which were there in case….'

Victoria stared at her. 'I understand.' Perhaps all the stuff they said about her great uncle Vittorio was true after all.

'When you wrote and said you were coming, I thought I'd better hide them,' Guiditta said. 'I didn't think you would want them or want to know about them. I thought … I thought you wouldn't understand.'

You might have been right about that, Victoria thought. 'OK. So you decided to hide them?'

'Yes. I didn't want you to think, well, I….' Guiditta stopped, and then burst out, 'There was nothing wrong, your great uncle was a good man, he was always good to me. I never saw him do anything wrong.'

Victoria realized that Guiditta was trying to protect her great uncle's reputation.

'Of course not. There was no reason why he shouldn't have kept guns if he wanted to.'

'No. I mean ... yes. Anyway, before you arrived I hid them in the attic out of the way. Now I'm thinking we might need them.'

'Yes. Is there any ammunition?'

'Plenty. In boxes with the guns.'

'I wonder if the guns are still there? Perhaps the Germans have found them by now.'

'I shouldn't think so,' said Guiditta. 'Why would they be looking in the attic? And I hid them well, wrapped up and behind some boxes. I put the ammunition in the bottom drawers of an old desk that's up there, right at the back. You wouldn't find them unless you were searching.'

By the time Victoria reached the villa, she had almost changed her mind. Although she and Guiditta had been over the plan again and again, trying to foresee every eventuality, she was very aware something could go wrong. Perhaps the guns weren't worth the risk ... but perhaps they were.

Her mouth was dry as she tried to attract someone's attention. There was no one on the reception desk in the large hall but the villa seemed to be busy, and as she waited, a platoon of soldiers pushed past her in an obvious rush, without even a glance in her direction. She watched as they clambered into waiting vehicles and drove off. Something seemed to be going on.

'What are you doing here?'

She turned to see the desk was now occupied. The soldier was viewing her with frank suspicion.

'Oh, hello,' Victoria said brightly. 'I was just waiting for you. I wondered if I could have a word with Oberst Fleischer please, if he could spare me a moment'

'Herr Oberst is very busy. Perhaps I can help you?' His manner intimated that the answer would be 'No' whatever the request.

'Perhaps I could wait?'

Before he could reply, the door to Fleischer's office opened and a harassed looking officer emerged, followed closely by Fleischer himself. He stared suspiciously at Victoria and then said 'What is your business here? We are very busy.'

'I'm so sorry, it won't take a minute. Just a small request.'

A curt nod and she was following him into his office. *No ... my great uncle Vittorio's drawing room....*

'What is it?' His tone was waspish, disinterested.

'You were so kind the other day, asking about the cottage, and I wondered –'

'You want to move back here?'

'Oh no! Er ... I mean, not at present thank you, but we have so little at the cottage and I wondered if I could collect some of our bedding from the attic? It was put away there when you arrived.'

'It would be much simpler for you to move to more comfortable quarters here.' A half smile briefly crossed his face.

'Perhaps.' Victoria faltered. 'May I think about it? In the meantime....'

His face had closed again. 'Do not take too long.' He strode to the door. 'Miss Vetti has permission to take some bedding from the attic,' he barked at the Gefreiter, who sprang to attention. 'Give her any help she needs.'

He retreated into his office again, and Victoria breathed out. She smiled her most winning smile at the officer. 'That will be lovely. There's an old pushchair in the garden room I can use, shall we get it?'

Half an hour later, Victoria reached the cottage with the old pushchair in tow. Guiditta was waiting with the door open, her apprehension apparent. As Victoria approached, she murmured, 'Be careful, Giorgio is here.'

'Giorgio?' Victoria composed her smile. She had only met her distant relative a couple times, but because of his reputation he always made her nervous. Now, as she entered the kitchen he rose from the armchair and gave her a peck on the cheek.

'Cousin,' he said lightly, and looked beyond her at the pushchair. 'Can I give you a hand with that?' His Italian was heavily accented, like Guiditta's, a breath of Naples here in Rome. As he wrestled the pushchair indoors, Victoria looked sharply at Guiditta and saw the slight flush there.

'You told him?' Victoria breathed. It was an accusation.

'He wanted to know why you were at the villa! It's alright, he's on our side.' Guiditta whispered.

There was a look of amusement on Giorgio's face as he surveyed the pushchair.

'You got them out, cousin?'

Victoria reached beneath the piled bedding and pulled out the hunting rifle. She handed it to Giorgio, who smiled his slightly crooked smile.

'You were brave, cousin, to take these from under their noses and of course, I know why you did it. How did you get them out? Didn't they search the pushchair?'

'Oh yes, but I wrapped them really well and then got the Gefreiter to help me. I swamped him with big bundles of sheets which he managed to drop, and I got the important bits into the pushchair while he was sorting it all out. I kept talking all the time and getting in the way. He was trying to get rid of me....'

Giorgio laughed out loud. 'Well done, cousin, this will be very useful. What else?'

Victoria realized she was going to lose the guns. She carefully uncovered the rest of the cache and the boxes of ammunition. She said, 'We need them for protection if and when the Boche decide to retreat.' She hesitated. 'I did not steal them for you.'

Giorgio loaded the rifle and raised it, peering down the sight. 'You did not steal them at all. They were Vittorio's property and now they are yours. The villa and all that it holds is yours. Don't forget that, cousin.'

He sat back down in the armchair and surveyed the two women. He was not a particularly large man, but had a certain presence, a swarthy but powerful demeanor. Not bad looking, regular features and penetrating dark eyes, but now Victoria thought of a phrase her mother sometimes used: *'You wouldn't want to meet him on a dark night'*.

He just smiled again, showing even teeth, and said, 'Is there any of that good coffee left? The stuff the American brought?'

Guiditta got stiffly to her feet. 'Yes. And there is some for you too, Victoria.'

So Guiditta must have told him about Guy's visit, unless he knew already, of course. He always seemed to know everything. She glanced at him again, but Giorgio did not speak until the coffee had arrived and he had taken a sip.

'I know why you stole the guns, cousin.' He leaned towards her. 'Of course you need protection here, do you think I would leave you with nothing? But what do you know of guns?' He smiled at her kindly. 'What you each need is one of these....' He picked up the handguns and examined them carefully. 'I will teach you how to load and use them before I go. But these....'

He picked up the shotguns and the rifle, and then a heavy revolver, weighing them carefully. 'These will help to get rid of the filthy Boche,' he said quietly.

'Well, I suppose … if you need them....' Victoria was dubious. Could you trust a known Mafioso?

'Do you realize…?' Giorgio's voice remained quiet. 'Do you realize, cousin, that in the city over three hundred people went missing last week after the bomb attack in the Via Rasella? No one knew what happened to them, there were many rumors but nothing definite. Then a few days ago there was an announcement in Il Messaggero, it said they were all shot. There were over thirty Germans killed in the bomb attack, and they took hostages and killed them – ten hostages for every German killed.'

Victoria faltered. 'How dreadful. We didn't know, we don't get any news here '

'Are you sure?' Guiditta had her hands to her face. 'How could they do that?'

Giorgio grimaced. 'I'm sure, yes. Some priests have been investigating and have found bodies. The stench led them to the Ardeatine Caves, where our forbears have lain in peace and tranquility for centuries. Now the place is desecrated by this terrible thing, and it is on the lips of everyone in Rome.' He fingered the shotguns gently. 'You must trust these guns to me, they are needed for what is coming and will be put to good use.' He raised his head and his eyes met Victoria's. 'What do you think Vittorio would have done?'

The question hung in the air. Victoria realized she had no idea what her great uncle would have done. She had no knowledge of him at all, whereas Giorgio and Guiditta had known him well. She knew only that he had been deported from the United States for his Mafia activities, and had left her the lovely villa.

If Vittorio was alive now, would he welcome the American invaders or support the Germans against them?

'I know what he would have done,' Guiditta said firmly. 'Your great uncle had a quarrel with the United States but he was no *fascista*. He would have deplored this terrible act against innocent people, and would have fought to get rid of the Boche.'

'Of course,' Victoria said. 'Take the guns and welcome, and we'll appreciate your help with learning to handle these.'

'Good,' said Giorgio. 'And when your brother gets here you can impress him with your expertise.'

He laughed at the look on Victoria's face. 'Didn't I tell you? Your brother and his friend are on their way here. That's why I came.'

By the time Giorgio had finished, Victoria realized that perhaps things were really beginning to move at last. Giorgio could tell them little of James's plans, only that he must see her, and it must be in secret. She had wondered whether it would be possible for Guy to repeat his visit in his previous guise, but Giorgio ruled this out as being too risky.

'They must come at night,' he said. 'This cottage can be seen from the villa, and you know yourself that you are watched. It will still be risky at night, but if they wait until it is really dark –'

'No!' Victoria said urgently. 'There is a better way.' Her face was shining. 'I only just realized ... we have been making plans, Guiditta and I. Plans for our own survival after the Germans leave, or if things become difficult.'

'What plans?' Giorgio's tone was wary.

'There is a cave, not large but well hidden, at the bottom of the field.' She gestured to the rear of the cottage. 'I have been taking basic stuff there, food and water, and blankets, and I was going to take the guns there as well. I have just realized it would be the ideal place for James and Guy to hide if they come here. They don't need to come to the cottage or use the road at all. They can approach across country. As you say, the last part will be in the dark, and I doubt they will be seen.'

Giorgio remained wary. 'I don't want you to get involved in their problems. I think you had better show me this cave.'

Victoria nodded. 'As soon as it gets dark.'

'And in the meantime,' said Giorgio, 'I will instruct you in the use of these handguns.'

When it was dark enough, Victoria and Giorgio left the cottage and made their way through the small garden and over the fence to the field. It was difficult to see where they were going, but Victoria had done the journey several times now, and led Giorgio unerringly through the field and along the left bank which overhung the cave. Giorgio was impressed as they made their way in, and Victoria switched on her torch.

'This is ideal,' he said. 'It's very well hidden. Are you sure the Boche haven't seen you?'

'I'm sure. If they had, Fleischer would have questioned me today, not let me walk out with bed linen.'

Giorgio smiled and nodded. 'You are becoming quite devious Victoria. You must have inherited it from Vittorio.' His voice changed, and he added quietly, 'I am a little concerned. I do not see any immediate problems, but you must remember that your brother and his friend are at war, and I do not want you involved in anything which will get you into trouble with the Germans. They do not know you are an American citizen and they must not find out. You must promise me not to take any risks.'

'My brother would not expose us to any risks,' Victoria replied. 'And anyway, I know you are my cousin, well at least my relative, but I do not have to promise you anything. I will always do what I think is right, for myself and Guiditta.'

Giorgio sighed. 'I am not trying to give orders here, Victoria, but I promised your great uncle I would look out for you if you ever came here. That is why I take an interest.'

'Really? I did not know that.' Victoria felt a little confused. 'I thought when I came here at first, and found out about you, that you would perhaps resent me?'

'Why should I do that?'

'Because Vittorio left me the villa, and I thought he should have left it to you. You were just as close a relative as me, and knew him well.'

Giorgio laughed. 'Don't worry, he left me plenty!' He patted her arm. 'Vittorio had several businesses, good ones, which I ran for him. He left them all to me. He left the villa to you because you were Paolo's daughter. He loved your father very much.'

'Yes, I see.' She didn't fully understand, but she knew he was right. Her mother had often talked to her about her handsome father, Paolo, who had been killed before she was even born, and who had sent her mother long-stemmed red roses on every birthday. James remembered him too, and had often talked of the young dark Italian who called him "little brother" and had played games and taken him for treats when he was growing up. She had never understood the whole story, but knew that when her parents were killed, Vittorio, her only living relative, had asked her parents to take care of her, knowing she would be safe with them.

She turned to Giorgio. 'I'm sorry if I seem ungrateful. I know Vittorio had my best interests at heart, and thank you for coming to tell us about what has happened in Rome, and about James. You don't know what it means to me to know he is alive.'

Giorgio did not reply, but he took her arm and led her to the mouth of the cave. As they emerged, a pale moon came from behind a cloud, providing a silvery grey light as Victoria extinguished the torch.

'I will tell James about the cave, and give him directions,' said Giorgio. 'Come here each evening from tomorrow when it is dark, to check if they have arrived. I don't know exactly when they will be here, they do not make me privy to their plans. Now go, quickly and carefully, and I will make my way across the field. No need to get the Boche excited.'

He gave Victoria a quick peck on the cheek and within seconds, he was gone.

CHAPTER EIGHT

The next day seemed interminable, as Guiditta and Victoria found themselves watching for James and Guy to make their appearance. It was ludicrous, because they knew the men would arrive only at night and would try to remain hidden. Even so, both women found themselves drawn again and again to the window, or the tiny garden, where their eyes raked the fields in hope of catching sight of some movement. None came, and on the first evening after Giorgio's visit, Victoria left the cottage as soon as she reasonably could, and returned only thirty minutes later, to say that there was no sign of the men at the cave.

'Of course not,' Guiditta consoled her. 'Giorgio has hardly had time to see them yet. They'll be here as soon as they can.'

'I know.' Victoria knew she was being impatient. 'It's just that it's been nearly three years since I saw James, and I've been worried about him.'

Guiditta smiled indulgently. She had no reason to doubt that Victoria was indeed very fond of her brother, but she suspected that Guy was on her mind as well.

'Yes, and I expect you'll be anxious to see Guy again too,' she ventured.

Victoria flushed, but she only said, 'Of course, it will be good to know he is safe. It's very dangerous out there for both of them.'

In fact, Guy and James were in no particular danger. After a tight-lipped parting from Chiara they had left the farmhouse, and had been shepherded across the mountainous countryside for several hours before being housed once again with an old farmer in an isolated cottage. He seemed delighted to have the company. He provided a tasty vegetable stew, and his only disappointment was that James could not give him much information about what was happening in the city. He seemed unable to comprehend the fact that just because James spoke perfect Italian, it did not necessarily mean he had anything to say.

'We know nothing,' James repeated for the umpteenth time. 'We have heard rumors that the partisans have been active in Rome, but we know no details at all. We are hiding, so we have no way of finding out anything, only rumors.'

The old man snorted. 'When you are up here all alone,' he said, 'even rumors are better than nothing.'

James laughed and spent a happy hour telling the old man about life in New York, which he exaggerated in every way he could just to watch the old man's eyes widen and twinkle with surprise or disbelief.

Eventually, it was time to leave, and they stumbled out onto the dark hillside, catching their feet in unexpected changes of level and clumps of brush and stones. It was hard going, as they could see very little, and they made slow progress for over an hour until the old man left them. He pointed out a shadowy building in the distance, which he told them was "the Boche HQ".

'The cave you want is at the back of that building. It's an old villa they have taken over, and there's a field at the back where the bank has an overhang. That's where you'll find your cave.' The words were almost a repetition of those Giorgio had used when he had given them instructions, and James and Guy thanked him before striking out alone. It was a dark night, but as they neared the edge of the field which bordered the villa grounds, a sliver of moon appeared briefly from behind the clouds and gave them a glimpse of the overhang at the edge. They made their way towards it, crouching and moving as quickly as possible. Half an hour later, they arrived at the cave.

They were delighted to find the candle Victoria had left there, together with water and a couple books.

'Thought you might like something to read' said the note attached to them.

James smiled, but gathered a blanket around himself and lay down. Guy picked up a book and glanced through it. Victoria …Victoria had left it there....

'I might read a little,' he said, lying down as well.

Within five minutes, both of them were asleep.

Looking out of the back window was again a main preoccupation for Victoria and Guiditta the next day, but Victoria was also increasingly drawn to the front of the cottage, where she could see what seemed to be increased activity to and from the Villa Vetti.

'I can't think what is going on,' she said for the second time. 'I've never seen it so busy. Soldiers leaving in big trucks – come and see.' As Guiditta joined her, she added, 'I thought perhaps they were leaving, but that's not it. Some are coming back again.'

'They will no doubt be very edgy, after what they have done with those hostages.'

They watched as the soldiers jumped down from a truck and lined up in the driveway. After a few moments they were dismissed, and walked slowly back into the villa.

'They don't look particularly happy,' said Guiditta. 'Do you think any of these men were involved in the shootings?'

'Possibly. But it could be that they know the Allies will not be long, perhaps they're getting nervous.'

'They should be nervous!' said Guiditta vehemently. 'They should be damned well ashamed of all they have put us through!'

'Well,' Victoria ventured quietly, 'it was Mussolini himself who joined up with Hitler, and when Italy surrendered, I suppose the Germans felt Italy was their enemy.'

Guiditta snorted. 'Mussolini! Mussolini!' She almost spat out the name. 'That upstart! We did not all agree with him, you know.'

Victoria did know. She had been made well aware of Guiditta's political leanings and her disdain for the former Italian leader, and knew what was coming next.

'Garibaldi! Now, there was a leader! Someone who put Italy first. My parents used to speak of him....'

Victoria switched off and returned to the kitchen, where a moment later Guiditta found her scraping a few small turnips. She sat down.

'They will come soon,' she said consolingly. 'Perhaps today even, as soon as it is possible.'

'Perhaps.' Victoria turned. 'I could go out looking for mushrooms again. They are used to me roaming the field....'

'Better to wait until tonight. Giorgio said we mustn't take the smallest risk.'

Victoria turned back to the sink. *Giorgio! What does he know? Is he even trustworthy?* She was aware that Guiditta trusted him, but that was because she had lived her whole life in the service of the Mafioso, the so-called Amici. She saw nothing wrong in their activities, it was just how things were.

And still are, she thought. It was all so confusing.

Victoria squatted on the ground, unable to take her eyes from those of her brother who sat opposite, skillfully opening a can with his army knife in the light of the two guttering candles which lit the cave. The skillet was already on the small fire and as James tipped up the can, the beans slid obediently into it, beginning to sizzle almost immediately.

'There you are,' James said proudly. 'We dip some of that hard tack into it and have a meal fit for a king. Who said Army K rations are boring?' He looked up and met her eyes, and began to laugh at her expression. 'What?'

'This is amazing.' Victoria laughed too. 'At home I never saw you so much as pick up a can, never mind cook something.'

'Never had to at home. Anyway, it was more a matter of principle.' He turned to Guy who was sitting on a box, allowing the siblings their moment. 'When you are brought up in a home where all anyone talks about or thinks of is food, you have to either become a chef too, or opt out altogether. I opted out.'

'Just like my home,' Guy said.

'Really?' Victoria was interested. Her heart had skipped a beat when she first saw him, and she still felt a little warm and excited. She smiled. 'Does your family run restaurants too?'

Guy shrugged. 'No, but we talked about food all the time. Usually, it was about where the next meal would come from, or how long it was since the last one.'

He clearly expected them to laugh, but they didn't.

'Sorry,' Victoria said.

'Hey! It was a joke … we never actually starved. Look, I'm still here, and as big and healthy as any other GI.'

Victoria smiled and James said, 'Well, at least we are all here, and together, and that seems something of a miracle. I had hoped we could meet up, but I didn't really expect it to happen.'

'Until it had to….' Guy supplied.

James sighed, but took the hint. 'To be honest, Vicky, we are here under orders.'

She grew wary. 'I don't understand. Giorgio said you wanted to see me, but –'

'Look, Vicky, this is top secret, and the less I tell you the better. I came into Rome to investigate the German organization here, so we will know what to expect and can target more efficiently. I've already sent back quite a lot of information, but we need to know more about this northern HQ at the villa. How many troops, that sort of thing, and even more important, what their plans are.'

'Their plans?'

'For the retreat.'

'You think they will be retreating soon? The Allies will be here soon?'

'No. Not necessarily. We have been bogged down and still are. But it is inevitable ... eventually.'

'How can you find out their plans?'

'By a covert operation, and for that we need your help. As you actually own the villa, you can gain access –'

'Me? You must be joking! I try to keep out of the way of Fleischer, he –'

'I know.' James's tone was soothing.

'You don't know! He is a real lecher, and wants me to go back and live there again.'

'Does he? That's useful.'

'You can't mean it! You can't want me to go back there?'

'I don't want you to do anything that would put you at risk,' James said. 'But we should discuss it, and see what is possible.' James lifted the pan of beans from the fire. 'Come on, guys, let's eat and think about it at the same time.'

Victoria was away so long that Guiditta had become apprehensive, responding to every small sound nervously. 'I thought something had gone wrong,' she fussed as Victoria quietly opened the kitchen door. 'I take it they were there?'

'Yes, they were there.' Victoria sank onto the old couch.

'So nothing has gone wrong? All is safe?'

'I wouldn't go as far as that. I have a lot to tell you.'

When it came down to it, the plan was fairly simple in essence. Victoria would tell Fleischer she had thought about his offer and had decided to move back to the villa with Guiditta. Once there, she would find out what she could, but more importantly, as she would be living on the top floor, she could arrange access for James and Guy to enter at night by the attic window. They knew what they were looking for, and would be able to go through the cabinets in Fleischer's office while he was asleep, and take or copy anything useful. If force had to be used, they would make it look like a partisan attack.

As she explained all this to Guiditta, Victoria's apprehension grew. It had seemed possible when they were discussing it in the cave, but now….

'I understand.' Guiditta interrupted her thoughts. 'You mean you could open a back bedroom window at night and they could get in that way.'

'Well, yes, if the guard isn't too lively.'

'But it's the front entrance that has the twenty-four hour guard, isn't it?' Once she had become used to the idea, Guiditta warmed to her theme. 'Once Fleischer has gone to bed, his office is locked and not used again until morning. Not usually, anyway. And Fleischer's bedroom is on the far side, so when they get in it probably won't wake him.'

'No, but it might wake the front guard,' said Victoria. She stared. 'Are you approving this mad scheme? I thought you would try to talk me out of it.'

Guiditta shrugged. 'I wouldn't mind having a go at those bastards,' she admitted. 'Anything is better than sitting out the rest of the war with a bad leg waiting to be shot or bombed.'

Victoria sighed. Three against one made it inevitable.

When she was at last in the small bed in the room she shared with Guiditta however, she did not worry about the details of their plan. Instead she allowed herself to drift away into a hazy dream where she was in Guy Waldman's arms, and she was looking into his eyes, and they were full of love....

CHAPTER NINE

James had emphasized that time was short, insisting Victoria should contact Fleischer the next day if possible. Because of this she woke early, putting her romantic dreams away and trying to concentrate on the plan. Could the information they were seeking be so important? If there was any information, of course ... and if they could gain access to it. She thought for a long time about how she would go about it, what might work and what would not, until her ideas became more and more confused. Eventually they lost any sort of reality, and only flitted through her mind in broken fragments which she could not catch or pin down.

When morning came, she was jittery as she prepared a frugal breakfast.

'I just don't know if it is the right thing to do,' she said for the tenth time.

Guiditta snorted. 'Of course you don't. What does that have to do with anything? Do you think anyone in this blasted war knows what they are doing and whether it is the right thing? You do what you have to, in order to survive.'

'We probably stand a better chance of survival if we keep our heads down,' Victoria snapped. 'What if Fleischer realizes what we are doing? He's no fool.'

'At least we may eat a little better at the villa,' Guiditta said, eyeing her crust of bread with disgust. 'If we stay here much longer we shall certainly not survive.'

'You mean you'd rather get shot than starve?' Victoria could not help but smile. She leaned across the table to Guiditta. 'Do you really think we can do it? Get James and Guy into the villa and out again without them finding out?'

Guiditta met her eyes. She was not accustomed to deep thinking and didn't like being forced to do it, preferring to watch others make a mess of things and even then reserve her judgment. She took a while to answer.

'I don't know if we can do it, any more than you do. But we can try, and you have to ask yourself how you will feel if we don't even try.'

Victoria sighed. 'I'll go up to the villa right away, before I lose my nerve.'

As she walked up to the villa Victoria reminded herself that she had been here only a few days before, so she knew what to expect and had nothing to worry about. That consolation was quickly proved wrong. The villa was bustling with soldiers who hardly gave her a glance, whereas usually the sight of a good looking young woman would at least bring a greeting and a smile. The Gefreiter on the desk was harassed, and waved her dismissively away when she asked to see Oberst Fleischer.

'Too busy,' he snapped.

'I only wanted to see him for a moment,' Victoria insisted. 'He asked me to come,' she added, wondering if this was in fact true.

The Gefreiter sighed, but waved her to a seat. 'Wait,' he said shortly.

Victoria wondered why everyone was in such a bad mood. She watched as scowling men approached the desk and were dealt with by the short-tempered Gefreiter. She sat there for almost three hours, as soldiers came and went. Try as she could, her German was not good enough to pick up what was happening, although it was obvious that something was going on.

The Gefreiter suddenly spoke to her. 'Oberst Fleischer will see you now,' he said, putting down the phone.

Fleischer was also in a bad mood.

'What is it?' he snapped, without the customary greeting.

'I'm sorry to trouble you, but when we last met you asked if Guiditta and me would like to move back here.'

She stopped. He was staring at her as if he had no idea what she meant. Then he shook his head slightly as if to clear his thoughts. 'Well?'

'We would appreciate it; the cottage is not very comfortable.' When he did not respond she added, 'If the offer is still open, of course.'

'Really?' She could not mistake the slight sneer. 'And what has brought on this amazing change of mind?'

'Well, it isn't a change of mind exactly,' Victoria said brightly. 'I wanted to accept before, but Guiditta's leg has been the problem. It's much better now though, and she tells me she thinks she can make the stairs.'

'Oh.' He thought for a moment and then nodded. 'I don't see why not. But things are very busy here....'

'Yes, I saw they were when I arrived. What on earth is going on?' She shrank before his withering look. 'I'm sorry; I didn't mean ... I only meant ... we don't get to know anything at all....'

'Not much to know,' he snapped. 'You may move in tomorrow if you wish, to the attic floor as you had before. I shall expect you to keep to your quarters and shall not expect to see you in any other part of the house.'

'Understood,' she said with a smile. 'But will you allow me access to the vegetable garden? I don't think there is much of anything there now, but there may be a few old greens we can salvage, or a few carrots….'

He nodded again. 'Very well.'

Victoria shuddered inwardly but forced herself to smile pleasantly and thank him. As she left the room he added,

'You may draw one small loaf of bread from the kitchen each day. I will inform the cook.'

Victoria could not disguise her genuine pleasure. 'Oh, thank you, Herr Oberst,' she said, and almost ran back to the cottage to tell Guiditta.

Because it was the last night they would spend in the cottage, Victoria knew she must visit the cave to let James and Guy know what had happened. Once they were living in the villa, it would be difficult to make contact. As soon as it was dark she made her way down to the cave. James jumped up and hugged her, and after a fleeting hesitation, Guy hugged her too. Victoria was overwhelmed by the torrent of emotion their closeness engendered. She sat down carefully on the blanket James had spread, and tried not to meet Guy's eyes. Was it the same for him? Surely she was not feeling this alone?

'We've made some coffee,' James said. 'It's not good, but better than anything you can buy in Rome. We saved you some.' He poured the dark liquid from the small pan into a tin cup and handed it to her. 'What's the news?'

'We are moving back to the villa, to the top floor, and we can have one small loaf every day from the kitchen.'

Guy and James exchanged a glance. 'Beware the Boche bearing gifts,' Guy said quietly. 'What else?'

'Nothing. I asked if we could use the garden vegetable plot and he said yes. There's nothing in it, but it is at the very bottom of the garden and I thought it would be a way for you to get access to the house. It has a high hedge so you could come up to that and I could perhaps make a hole for you to get through. Not noticeable, of course....'

James was smiling. 'Vicki, you are turning into a real little partisan, but don't take any risks. I think we can about manage to make a hole in a hedge. When do you move in?'

'Tomorrow. I'm not looking forward to it. Something is going on and everyone was in a really foul mood, including Fleischer.'

James smiled again. 'We had better make sure our plans are properly laid then, hadn't we?'

CHAPTER TEN

It was, in fact, hardly a "move" at all. The women had few personal possessions at the cottage and these were easily accommodated in the old pushchair and taken to the villa. By ten o'clock next morning, when they were ready to depart, the back door opened to reveal Giorgio, out of breath and carrying a small paper bag which he threw onto the table. He nodded to Victoria, and then at the bag.

'Don't get excited, there's nothing in it.' He smiled widely. 'If you are asked why I was here, I brought you a few vegetables from the mountains. And before you ask, yes, they have seen me ... I waved to them!'

'But why are you here?' Victoria was astonished by his sudden appearance.

Giorgio had now slumped onto the old couch. 'To stop you doing this insane thing. I told you not to get involved in this prank of your brother's –'

'Prank? It's not a prank!'

'Well, whatever it is, you don't have to be part of it,' Giorgio insisted. 'Let your brother do his thing, no matter how daft or misguided it is, but you stay out of it. Moving back into the villa is asking for trouble.'

Victoria stared at him. *How did he know? The plans were only made last night, yet here he is, shouting the odds, giving orders....* A sudden chill ran through her. She knew Giorgio had his spies, but this was ridiculous.

'How did you know we were moving?' she said coldly.

Giorgio tapped his nose. 'By now, cousin, you should have realized that I know everything. Always!'

They had been speaking in fast Italian, and Guiditta, who had been following the conversation closely, chuckled at this, highly amused.

'It's not funny!' Victoria snapped. 'If he knows our plans already, it doesn't say much for our security, or our chances of success. If Giorgio knows, the Boche may know as well....'

'Easy ... easy.' Giorgio was leaning forward, his tone conciliatory. 'First, Victoria, I do not know your plans, only that you are to move back to the villa. Second, from that I surmise that this must be something to do with some operation of your stupid brother, who needs you to be inside the villa to assist him –'

'My brother is not stupid!' Victoria said angrily.

'Then it may be you who is stupid to agree to his silly war games.' Giorgio was becoming angry himself, but he tried again. 'Victoria, please. I am thinking only of you and Guiditta. Do not put yourselves in danger ... please.'

'Thank you for your advice, but I am capable of making my own decisions,' Victoria responded. Her face was closed and her mouth set. It was Guiditta who intervened.

'Giorgio,' she said gently, 'we have discussed our plans very carefully and in detail with James and Guy. We know what we are doing and have considered the danger. Nobody is stupid, we have decided to do something to help this war towards an end, if we can.'

'Enough said. I tried my best.' Giorgio hauled himself out of the old couch and made for the door, where he stopped. 'Don't ask me for help if it all goes wrong, that's all.' He opened the door and then turned back. 'I did not mean that. If you need help, ask a man called Paolo.' He smiled briefly. 'Same name as your father, Victoria. He works at the villa, does odd jobs and also helps in the kitchen. Do not speak to him unless it is an emergency.'

So that is how he knew we were moving in! He's obviously had a spy in the villa all this time and didn't even tell me! How can I trust this man?

Aloud, Victoria said, 'Giorgio, you will not do anything, will you? To stop James? Or sabotage our plans?'

She watched the shock register on his face. It was as if he had been slapped.

'That … that question does not deserve an answer.' He went out and closed the door behind him.

Guiditta was staring in shock. 'How could you?' she rasped. 'How could you say such a thing to him, after all he has done for us?'

'All he has done for us? What has he done for us? What?'

'Sent us food when he could, watched our backs –'

'Having a spy in the villa without even telling me? You call that "watching our backs"?'

'Of course it is.' Guiditta was furious now. 'Why do you think he was there? To watch the Germans to see how they peel their potatoes? Do you think Giorgio would put a spy there if the villa did not belong to you? Really Victoria, you make me very angry sometimes!'

Could she have gotten it so wrong? Guiditta obviously thought so. Had she really offended Giorgio? Was it possible to offend someone like him? He was a known Mafioso … or Amici … or whatever they wanted to call it. She had tried to understand, and had tried to explain it to Guy when they discussed it, but it was all very confusing. One thing she did know, she trusted Guiditta.

'I'm sorry if you think I offended him,' she said slowly. 'I know you believe you can trust him, but I have difficulty with … with the fact that he is….'

'I know, I know. You watch too many gangster movies in America. Your ideas of Mafia come from there, not from here.' Guiditta warmed to her theme. 'All to do with money, everything in America is to do with money. You understand nothing else.'

'That's not true, Guiditta. I do understand about loyalty, and friendship. I am so sorry; we seem to be having our first row. I do not know Giorgio as you do, but I trust you, and if you say he is OK then I will try to trust him too.'

Guiditta appeared slightly mollified by this. She sighed, and then said, 'We had better wait an hour before we go. Then if someone asks why Giorgio came here, we can explain he brought vegetables, and we already ate them.'

Victoria smiled ruefully. 'OK, and you are sure the handguns are well hidden? Just in case they should search our stuff when we arrive?'

'Oh, they are well hidden, can you see them?'

'No.' Victoria was mystified. In answer, Guiditta lifted her voluminous black skirt to reveal her naked legs, one still dressed with grubby strapping around and above the knee. It was obvious the leg was still swollen.

'Oh gosh! You have one in there?'

'And the other in my corset. I don't think they will look there.' Guiditta laughed. 'Perhaps if I was eighteen....'

In the cave, the hours seemed to crawl for James and Guy. They had planned and re-planned, testing their theories against any possible eventualities and trying to foresee any problems. Guiditta's idea of trying to open the back bedroom window had long since been shelved as much too risky. There were too many possible German troops in too many possible places on the ground floor, even at night. The only place where the situation could be known was the attic flat where Victoria and Guiditta would be in residence. It was not really a flat, according to Victoria, just a large space already crowded with old furniture, but when she had first moved in there she had attempted to make part of it into a habitable area, and would do so again. The only real difficulty was water, which had to be carried up the steep staircase from the main house, and any cooking had to be done on an old two-ring camping gas appliance, for which refills were becoming increasingly difficult to obtain, along with everything else.

There was a window overlooking the side of the villa which seemed promising, as it could be opened by Victoria, but it was at least 20 feet from the ground. Nevertheless, the plan was based on entry being gained through this means, and James and Guy had discussed *ad infinitum* how it could be done, still with no result. They were discussing the possibility of making a harness from the combined straps from their back packs when a slight sound had them diving for cover. For a few seconds they remained frozen, listening intently, before they heard a whispered 'James? James Sullivan? It's OK. It's Giorgio. I'm coming in. Don't shoot....'

Seconds later Giorgio entered the cave, and as his eyes became accustomed to the gloom he saw that he was covered by two rifles aimed directly at him. He lowered his own gun slowly and put it on the ground. 'OK now ... we have not met before, but you know me, I am Victoria's cousin....'

Although his Italian was heavily accented, James understood him immediately and lowered his gun. He came forward and took Giorgio's hand.

'If you are Victoria's cousin, then I suppose we are cousins too.'

Giorgio's hard stare wiped the smile from James's face. He continued to stare for a few seconds before he said, 'No. No blood relation.'

'Well no, I understand that,' James responded coldly. 'But Victoria and I have been raised as brother and sister and –'

'That's OK then, as long as we understand, no blood relation for you and me.' He turned to Guy. 'Who is this?'

Guy held out his hand. 'Guy Waldman, Victoria has told me about you.'

It was a formality, but Giorgio considered it carefully before saying sourly, 'Ah yes. You are the one who visited her and *stayed overnight!*'

Guy was aghast. 'Hey, now....'

Giorgio smiled briefly. 'OK, OK, Guiditta was there, I know.' His eyes roamed around the small cave. 'Anything to drink?'

He seated himself on the only box as James said, 'Just water,' and poured some into a tin cup. For some reason Giorgio seemed to dominate the situation. He had already caught them both on the hop and had taken charge. James attempted to rectify this. He faced Giorgio squarely and demanded, 'How did you know we were here? Did Victoria tell you?'

Giorgio laughed. 'Of course not, but you are right, I have just come from seeing her.' He leaned forward. 'I am not happy. She is moving back into the villa and into danger. This is your doing. You say she is your sister, but if she was blood relation you would not do this.'

'How dare you! What has it to do with you? You have nothing to do with us, or what we do.' James stopped, and then retorted, 'I know you and your type, I expect you are doing well out of the occupation –'

Guy stepped between them as Giorgio leaped up, red-faced and snarling. Pushing Guy roughly aside, he threatened James with his fist and growled, 'I am not *fascista*! I hate these fucking Germans! But I am not partisan either, I do not make war on anybody!'

'Just make money out of whoever happens to be in power. I know your sort,' James sneered. 'You take advantage of anybody and everybody.'

'At least I do not use women to help me … like you do!' Giorgio swung on his heel. 'I came to ask you to be careful, to watch out for Victoria, to see if I could help. I can see I waste my time. Don't worry, Mr. American big guy, I will keep your little secrets, but if Victoria is harmed –' his eyes narrowed and his voice became menacing, '–I shall seek you out and kill you.'

He left the cave, and the Americans stared at each other in consternation.

CHAPTER ELEVEN

By the time the move to the villa was completed, the plans had also been finalized between Guy and James. Victoria had managed to make a quick visit to the cave on the pretext that she wanted to search for mushrooms, and confirmed this by showing her success to the Gefreiter on the desk when she returned. 'You see?' she said with a big smile, opening the small bag. 'It was worth the effort.'

For a moment Victoria thought he was about to smile back, but he couldn't quite make it. He inspected the few mushrooms briefly, and gave a curt nod. Victoria took her prize to the attic, where Guiditta was busy cleaning the handguns.

'You saw them?' she asked intently. 'Is it good news?'

Victoria sighed. 'I hardly know. I shall not be able to visit the cave again. They say it is too risky. Apparently Giorgio went to see them and made a fuss about us being involved.'

'I'm not surprised. He made it pretty clear to us what he thought.'

'Yes, but now James thinks we have to act immediately. He thinks it is safer to do that rather than delay, which might mean discovery.'

'That makes sense.' Guiditta hobbled to the table and put down the gun. 'What do you mean by immediately?'

'Tonight.'

'Tonight? Are they sure they are ready?'

'They seem to think so. The question is, are we?'

'All we have to do is open the window.'

Victoria gave a wry smile. 'That's not quite all. We have to get out and get away with them. We can't possibly stay here afterwards, they are sure to suspect we are involved.'

'But where shall we go?'

'It's arranged, apparently. We go into the partisan line that got James here. We only have to get to the cave; someone will be there to take us up into the hills.'

Guiditta looked horrified. 'But how shall I manage with my leg? I don't know that I can.'

'I know. It will be difficult. If our plan works and we get them in, and they are able to get the information they need, and we can all get away without anyone realizing what has happened, then it should be alright. If we can get away in the dark, we should be OK. If it all goes wrong, then it's anybody's guess.'

Guiditta nodded, her momentary panic over. 'We shall be OK,' she said. 'How are they going to get in?'

'There is a big trash can that they will move from the back to stand on. Let's hope they can move it quietly. They have made a kind of rope out of strapping from their back packs which should enable them to climb up the rest of the way. They will throw it up to us and we have to secure it. I had a look at it and it seems strong enough.'

'Better than the usual twisted sheets anyway,' Guiditta said, in an attempt at levity. 'What about that old dresser to hold it? We can move it to the window this afternoon, but it will take some shifting.'

Victoria agreed. 'Yes, ideal. Then we must pack just one small bag with only the most important items for us to take. I will carry it. Then I'll go down to the kitchen to see if we can have this "one small loaf" Fleischer promised. We can have mushrooms on toast. At least we shall have a meal before we go, we don't know when we shall get the next one.'

Two hours later, Victoria tapped on the kitchen door and entered. There were three men working there preparing food. One of them looked up and said, 'I will do it.' He went to a shelf which was piled with bread and took down a small loaf. He brought it across and held it out to Victoria.

'You are Miss Vetti?' he asked pleasantly, but did not wait for an answer. 'I am Paolo.' He held her eyes for a second. 'You are allowed one small loaf each day. Oberst Fleischer's orders.'

Victoria took the bread with a brief 'thank you,' as Paolo turned away. She glanced back as she closed the kitchen door, and saw that Paolo was already back at work, slicing carrots.

By ten o'clock that evening, the waiting was unbearable. Despite sitting with their ears to the outside wall, neither Victoria nor Guiditta heard anything. If the trash can was being moved it was being done very quietly. James had specified that at ten o'clock the window should be opened, and Victoria now did so, having carefully oiled the window catch and bolt earlier. It opened noiselessly and Guiditta nodded approval. 'It's probably the only window in the villa that still opens properly,' she said. Victoria chanced a peep below. Nothing. She shook her head at Guiditta and sat down to wait. Five minutes went by and then Victoria ventured another peep.

'Gosh, they're here!' she whispered. 'At least, the trash can is....'

Seconds later she saw a dark form standing on the top of the can, and heard the hoarse whisper, 'Catch!' She did, and found herself holding a shoe.

'Another!' Again she managed to catch it.

'Now the rope....'

This was more difficult, she missed at the first attempt, but whoever was at the bottom managed to catch it as it fell.

'Again!' This time she caught the tightly bound strapping, and unwound it carefully. She had expected to have to tie it on to the dresser leg, but there was a mountaineer's type hook and latch on the end, and Victoria soon had it fastened securely round the dresser and dangling down below. It seemed barely long enough, but the dark form latched on to it and began to climb, quickly and expertly. Within seconds Victoria was helping Guy over the window ledge. He seemed to take up all the space near the window as he took off his black knitted hat.

'Hi girls,' he whispered, blowing Guiditta a kiss. 'Now for James.' He lowered the strapping down from the window.

'Are there shoes again?' Victoria whispered.

'No, he has them in his pockets.'

Victoria was about to ask why Guy didn't put his shoes in his pockets when James's head appeared at the window. Guy helped him in silently, and he embraced Victoria.

Victoria closed the window. 'What now?' she asked, turning to face the others.

'So far, so good.' James said. 'Now we wait until around ten thirty and then you, Victoria, will go down to make sure Fleischer has gone to bed. You said he goes to bed early?'

'Yes. Well, he did when we were here before, unless there were other senior officers visiting, in which case it was drinking until all hours.'

'Let's hope there are no visitors then. And the guards on duty?'

'Are at the front, there were two earlier on, but I don't know how many now.'

James nodded and took a seat. 'Well, this is nice.' He looked around, perfectly relaxed, as if he had just called in for a cup of tea. He turned to Guiditta, and held out his hand. 'You must be Guiditta, we haven't met, but I've heard a lot about you.'

Guy's eyes rolled upwards. He couldn't help it could he? Always the same, fifteen or fifty, James just couldn't help laying on the charm.

He met Victoria's eyes briefly; she had noticed it too. They smiled, and there was an unspoken recognition, a private joke although neither had spoken.

Suddenly, James put his fingers to his lips. Victoria motioned to the men to hide. There had been a sound … the sound of the door at the bottom of the attic stairs opening, and now the heavy tread of footsteps.

There was no time to think. Victoria started quickly towards the stairs and gazed down in amazement at Fleischer, who was already a third of the way up.

He paused. 'Good evening, Miss Vetti,' he said pleasantly. 'I thought I would come to see if you are settled in comfortably.'

'How very kind of you,' Victoria said brightly.

'I was just retiring, but thought I would see if you had what you need.' He began to ascend the stairs further, but Victoria stepped down to meet him. 'We do have all we need, but Guiditta is just preparing for bed, so I'd prefer it if you didn't come up just now.'

As if in answer to her prayers, Guiditta appeared behind her, her blouse trailing, giving Fleischer a glimpse of a large tea-rose colored bra before she retreated quickly with a squeak.

Fleisher retreated too, and Victoria said, 'I'll follow you down, I wanted to see you anyway when you had a moment, to thank you for the bread....'

As they reached the bottom of the staircase Victoria turned on her winning smile. 'We collected our first loaf today, such good bread after what we have had lately.'

Fleischer seemed a little taken aback, but said hesitantly, 'I don't suppose you would care for a drink, Miss Vetti?'

'A drink? I certainly would. I haven't been offered a drink for months!' She smiled again. 'Lead on, Herr Oberst,' and she followed him across the large square hall to his private quarters.

In the attic, Guy and James breathed out. Guiditta sank onto the bed, pulling her blouse back on as the men turned away. As she fastened the buttons, Guy sat down beside her and patted her on the shoulder. 'That was some quick thinking on your part.'

James was a little shaken. 'Yes, and on Victoria's too. Who would have thought it? Do you think he'll make a pass at her?'

'Of course.' Guiditta gave him a withering look. 'You two had better act fast while she keeps him busy.'

'Has she got a gun?' Guy was upset at the prospect of Victoria having to deal with Fleischer's advances.

'Of course not, how could she hide one in those clothes?' Guiditta rose. 'I have one', she said, taking the small revolver from a drawer. 'And I'll take hers, too. I'll follow her down and make sure she's OK.'

'Right.' James was in command again. 'We'll start right away. As soon as we are finished we'll come back up here, this window is still the best way of escape.'

Paolo's nerves were on edge. What the hell was going on? Living every day with the constant threat of discovery, he was used to looking over his shoulder, but now he looked around the big kitchen with eagle eyes.

'If you finish the washing down, I'll do the trash,' he offered to Helmut, the other kitchen hand who was clearing away the last of the tin mugs from the troops' late drinks, which were always the last item of the day for the kitchen staff.

Helmut nodded listlessly, it had been a long day. Paolo began to gather the rubbish together. It was the same every night, after late drinks a last clean down and put out all the trash. The only problem was that the big trash bin had disappeared, as Paolo had noticed half an hour ago when he stepped out for a smoke. He knew immediately it was significant. Trash bins that size didn't just disappear, and he had been warned by Giorgio that something might be in the wind.

He opened the kitchen door and took out two full boxes of trash. He darted around the building and realized what was happening as soon as he saw the bin under the attic window. He grabbed it quickly and took it back to its normal place, moving as quietly as possible. He put in the two boxes and went back into the kitchen, to be met by Helmut carrying some more trash.

'I said I'd do the trash,' Paolo said.

'No problem, I'm finished now and this is the last. I shall be glad to get to bed.'

Helmut deposited the trash in the bin and came back inside, locking the kitchen door. He took out the door key and grabbed his coat from a peg.

'Come on,' he said, and they walked into the hall and down to the guard at the front entrance, where Helmut gave in the key.

'See you tomorrow,' Paolo said as he left the building and started to walk towards the stables, once housing for twenty horses, which was where the civilian staff now slept.

That was a narrow squeak, he mused. *How on earth can I get the bin back in place for when they want to get out?*

CHAPTER TWELVE

Victoria smiled graciously as Fleischer handed her a glass of wine. She had been surprised at the choice on offer. As well as wine, he had a good variety of spirits and beers, all well arranged on what had been her great uncle's dresser. The heavy old piece of furniture still stood in the same place in what used to be called the garden room. Guiditta had taken delight in polishing the lovely silver which used to be displayed there, but now the dresser had become a well stocked bar. Victoria was uncomfortably aware of the large double bed in the corner; this was now Fleischer's private quarters. It was still an elegant room, she thought, large and comfortable, with the beautiful French windows opening onto the garden, and the pictures on the walls still intact.

Doesn't matter, she thought, *the pictures aren't worth a lot. Whatever they say about my great uncle Vittorio, he didn't have much artistic taste; that I do know....*

She sipped her wine and looked up at Fleischer, wondering if she would be able to control this. *Just behave like a lady, and a man will behave like a gentleman....* As the wine flooded her tongue with a taste she had almost forgotten, she smiled appreciatively. 'This is good.'

'Yes, it is an Italian wine. I like the whites of Alsace myself, and did not think I would appreciate the wines in Italy, which I had never tried before I came here. They were a pleasant surprise, at least some of them.'

It was patronizing, but he smiled, and Victoria realized he really was trying to be friendly. *That's OK, as long as I can keep it at this level. Are they in*

the office yet? I wonder how long it will take them?
She strained her ears, but heard nothing. An idea came to her.

'I don't suppose you have any music?'

Fleischer crossed the room and stooped to a cupboard. He turned, a record in his hands.

'I have dance music,' he said almost triumphantly 'Do you like dance music?'

Glad to have found a way to distract him, she smiled in apparent delight as he put the record on. 'Oh, I love this, Herr Oberst. Turn it up a bit louder please, and we can dance....'

James and Guy were well into their task. After some horrifying moments, as they jemmied open the filing cabinets trying not to make a noise, James had quickly identified the one which held the main records.

'No time to sort it,' he whispered. 'Put all this in the back pack and I'll see if there is anything else.' His knowledge of languages stood him in good stead as he ransacked the records methodically and clinically. His knowledge of German was not so well developed as his Italian, but still it was adequate to the purpose. As Guy loaded files into the large back pack, he realized for the first time that James might be good officer material after all. Despite his flippancy, James knew exactly what he was doing here. Guy wouldn't have known where to start with this lot. Suddenly, some music sounded quite loudly from the direction of the hallway. They looked at each other and James smiled. 'Victoria is doing her stuff.'

'Let's get on with it,' Guy whispered. He didn't like this at all.

Paolo shivered. It was early in the season and the Spring evening air was crisp and quite cold. He bent double and kept to the edge of the garden which bordered the old stable area. He could not move too quickly as it was so dark, but as he neared the house he saw the lights were on in Fleischer's private rooms. A moment later, he saw Fleischer himself come to the French windows and close the heavy curtains, engulfing the terrace and lawn in darkness.

He waited for his eyes to adjust, until he could make out the kitchen door. He crossed the lawn quickly, his heart in his mouth, vaguely aware of dance music coming from the villa. What was going on? All he knew was that someone needed the bin to be back where they had left it….

Victoria was almost reeling from the strong stench of Fleischer's sweat as he clasped her even closer. His strength terrified her, and she attempted to pull away. But Fleischer had drunk a full bottle of wine and was not letting go, and she felt his mouth exploring her neck. *It is time to stop this, surely James and Guy have found what they wanted by now…?* She tried again, but Fleischer was steering her inexorably towards the bed, nuzzling at her as his hands roved down her back and over her buttocks. With a sudden hard push, she was on her back on the bed, gazing up at him.

'Herr Oberst,' she attempted, shaking her head. 'Just a moment … I do not want this….'

'Of course you do.' He was on top of her, his long cold fingers digging into her breast, as his other hand wrenched up her skirt. She tried to wriggle away but he was strong and determined.

'I said no!' She struggled to push him away. He stopped for a moment, giving Victoria time to sit up and pull down her skirt. Then, to her consternation, he started to laugh.

'Do you think you can do it again?' he snarled, and she saw the vicious look in his eyes. 'Do you think you can fob me off again? Like you did before? No, my dear Miss Vetti, it is time you came down to earth. You wanted to come and live here, and I allowed you to do so. You knew there would be a price to pay ... and what that price was.'

'No! I did not think there was a price. I thought, Herr Oberst, that you were a gentleman....'

He laughed again, a hard, disbelieving sound.

'Ha! A gentleman. Of course I am not! And you believed nothing of the kind. You thought I was a stupid German, a stupid Boche, isn't that what you call us? Well, you can have it which way you like, but you will have it. We can make an arrangement, as I offered before, a regular arrangement on my terms, or you can put up a fight and I will have the pleasure of taking what I want, when I want, with your agreement or not....'

Still she sought to retrieve ground. 'I cannot believe this; you have been so kind –'

'This pretence stops now! Yes, I have done all the giving and you have done the taking. Now it is your turn to give.' He snorted. 'Do you think you are the first? I can have as many girls as I want. Have you not realized, even now we are at war and you are on the losing side? Oh yes, there have been plenty of nice Italian girls who refused to have anything to do with the hated Boche ... until they got hungry enough. Now they plead to open their legs for a crust of bread or a bar of soap....'

He stopped suddenly and looked at her, and she saw the anger and determination behind his lizard-like eyes. 'So choose,' he said viciously. 'Pretend we are both civilized human beings, or fight me. Either way we have sex ... a lot of sex....'

He leered over her. 'I don't mind if you just pretend you like it,' he sneered. 'I'm not proud....'

Victoria found her voice. 'I will never sell myself for a loaf of bread a day,' she said.

'Ha! You'll never sell yourself at all! You have nothing to sell because I'm not buying. I'm taking.'

He pushed her down on the bed and in spite of her struggles she felt his hand groping between her thighs. In seconds her panties were being torn away. *My God! This can't be happening! No! I won't, you German bastard ... you disgusting ....Oh God, help me!*

With one arm across her body, pinning both her arms down, his other hand quickly unzipped his trousers. She felt the hard urgency of his body on her thighs. She screamed aloud and arched her back to try and prevent him....

The sudden blast shattered the air, and blood was spurting, Fleischer's blood, spurting all over her. *What is happening? What is he doing?* His body stiffened and jerked almost upright, his eyes staring as the blood pumped from him. Victoria fought to get away from the bloody weight which crashed down on her. Gasping in horror, she managed to roll him away and staggered upright, to see Guiditta in the doorway, still holding the handgun and pointing at the dead man as if she would shoot him again.

For a moment they stood and stared at each other, frozen in horror, and then they embraced, with tears of shock. A moment later, Victoria dragged Guiditta into the room as shouts resounded in the hallway. Her shaking hands turned the key in the lock and she ran to the French windows, opening them quickly.

'This way, we must get out this way' she ordered, almost calm in the tension of the moment.

Guiditta followed her out. The old lady was tremulous and frightened. 'What about Guy and James? They –'

'Never mind about them, they will have heard. Come on, Guiditta, come on….'

They scrambled across the terrace and ran blindly down the garden towards the far hedge, followed by the sound of splintering wood that told them the door to Fleischer's room was being demolished.

Like everyone else, Paolo had heard the shot, and within seconds he saw the two women fleeing over the lawn towards the open fields. He was confused … surely the women did not need the bin? There must be someone else in there…. He grabbed the big heavily-lidded bin and dragged it as fast as he could round to the side of the villa, replacing it under the attic window. Almost immediately the window opened, and he saw a man heave himself over the window ledge and climb down. Paolo waited till the man reached safety and then he raced away, but he had barely reached the far side of the lawn when he came face to face with a German soldier, who pointed a rifle at him and ordered him to stop.

Guy and James had been on the point of leaving the office when they heard the gunshot. James was not sure whether the information they had taken was what HQ required, but he did know that whatever information was held there, they had it. They left the office and immediately made for the attic stairs, hopeful that Victoria would meet them up there with Guiditta. By the time they found that neither of the women was there, it was too late to do anything but leave the villa by the attic window. They both scuttled as fast as possible down the rope and then through the side hedge and away into the fields, and as they did so another shot rang out, and a scream of pain.

'I must go back,' James said. 'Victoria may be trapped.'

'I'll come with you,' Guy said.

'No you won't, either of you!' said a sharp Italian voice behind them.

'Julio!' James thought he had never been so glad to see anyone in his life.

'The women are safe,' Julio said. 'I've sent them on down to the cave, but the Germans will be all over the place in minutes. If we can join them fast and get across the fields we might just make it....'

Even as he spoke lights were going on in the villa and a stream of armed soldiers began to cross the lawn.

'Go quickly!' said James. 'I'll stay and hold them off for a while....'

'No, I'll stay,' said Guy, but the look James gave him brooked no discussion. 'Your job is to get those files to HQ,' he said. 'And to get Vicki and

Guiditta to safety.' He nodded to Julio. 'Tell Chiara....'

Julio nodded back, but all hell was breaking loose and as James ran back to the hedge and began to fire, Guy and Julio turned and ran for their lives, gunfire exploding behind them.

CHAPTER THIRTEEN

Paolo lay back in the cold metal chair. His leg was bleeding profusely. *Why on earth did I try to run? They might have believed me if I had just played it out, pretended I'd heard the gunshot and was wondering what had happened....*

The Gefreiter, who had been on duty in the hall that afternoon, leaned over him. He was sweating heavily and obviously in a state of shock.

'What were you doing in the garden?' he asked for the third time. His Italian was hardly intelligible.

'Just what I told you, Sir. I heard a gunshot and was coming to see what happened....' Paolo's face was agonized. 'Please, sir,' he gasped in poor German, 'get me some help. I am bleeding to death....'

'Did you put the bin under the attic window?' The Gefreiter bent down and rammed his service revolver heavily onto Paolo's injured leg. The pain was excruciating and Paolo screamed. The German repeated the question.

'What?' Paolo gasped. 'What do you mean? What bin?' The pain in his leg was so bad he began to weep, he couldn't help it. 'Do you mean the big bin by the kitchen?'

'You know perfectly well what I mean. The bin you put under the attic window so the partisans could climb up to the attic, where your friend Miss Vetti let them in –'

'What do you mean? The bin was outside the kitchen when I went off duty, ask Helmut, he was there ... and I don't know Miss Vetti.'

Paolo grimaced in pain, but the Gefreiter tapped his revolver again onto the injured leg, causing waves of agony. 'Tell me the truth, and I will stop the pain and get you a doctor.'

Tears were coursing down Paolo's cheeks. 'I only met Miss Vetti today, when she came to the kitchen to get some bread ... it was Oberst Fleischer's orders.'

The Gefreiter was white with anger. He pressed the revolver hard down onto the wound. Paolo screamed again. 'What has happened?' he gasped. 'I don't understand. Is Miss Vetti dead?'

This seemed to infuriate the Gefreiter even further. 'If she isn't, she soon will be.' He put his face close to Paolo's and said quietly, 'She shot Oberst Fleischer ... with your help and that of the partisans who ransacked his office.'

Paolo's shock was genuine, and the Gefreiter, after a moment's hesitation, nodded to a guard, who went outside. Moments later the door re-opened and the guard, together with another soldier, carried in a bloody body and flung it at Paolo's feet. The corpse was riddled with bullets, but the blue eyes were still open and blond hair fell across the forehead in a casual way, almost as if the man were about to make a flippant remark.

'Do you know this man?' the Gefreiter rasped.

Paolo shivered and shook his head. 'I have never seen him before in my life.'

It was the truth. He had never met James Sullivan.

It seemed a never ending scramble across uneven ground in the dark. Several times Victoria felt ready to give up, especially when poor Guiditta was struggling so badly. Julio was helping her, at times practically carrying her, and Victoria tried to help as well, but the going was very hard and she had trouble keeping her footing as they hurried ever further from the villa. All she could think of was James, left behind to cover for them, so they could get away. What had happened to him? In her heart she knew it must be bad, it was unimaginable that he could have escaped from such a situation.

He had kept them at bay though; the soldiers who would have been hot on their trail had been mown down and then kept from their purpose for who knows how long? Victoria prayed that James had been taken prisoner, although if he had, it might be even worse for him after all the mayhem. She glanced across at Guy, struggling under the enormous back pack he carried, and as she saw his closed and drawn expression she knew that he too, feared the worst for his friend.

James was dead, she was sure of it, and they were all alive because he had given them time to get away ... she bit back her tears and struggled on.

It seemed like hours later, but it must have only been a little more than an hour, when there was suddenly a helping hand at her side and a sweet Italian voice asking, 'Are you OK? Come on, it's not far now ... just to the top road, there is a car waiting....'

Victoria grabbed hold of the young woman's hand and held on tightly; hardly noticing the girl herself as she painfully climbed the last thirty yards or so up to the narrow road which was waiting above them. *How on earth has Guiditta managed?* Glancing round, she saw that Julio had been released from his burden and that Guiditta was being stretchered up the mountainside by two sturdy men, with Julio scrambling up behind. Guy was already at the top, trying to divest himself of the huge back pack.

The moon had risen now and although it was a cloudy night, Victoria could see the car waiting on the road above, and felt tears spring to her eyes. How suddenly everything had changed ... what on earth were they doing here? She reached out and grasped Guy's hand as he reached down for her, and was enveloped in a bear hug. It was a hug of relief, but of sorrow too, and she did not know which of them was clinging the tightest, because the horror of everything was too close and would not go away. And then she heard a voice she knew, a voice which whispered, without its usual arrogance.

'Giorgio!'

He put his hands around her head and kissed her soundly on the cheeks. 'Thank God, cousin! Get in the car quickly; you must be far away by morning.'

He took charge, bundling Guiditta and herself into the back seat with the young woman, and Guy in the front passenger seat. The back pack went into the trunk. Victoria assumed he was going to drive, but instead a grizzled older man got into the driver's seat and Giorgio leaned in through the window.

'Giuseppe will drive you, you can trust him. Follow his instructions. We can get you much nearer to the Allied lines.'

'Aren't you coming with us?' Suddenly, Giorgio seemed a safe haven to Victoria, and she was amazed she had distrusted him.

'No, not yet, I must find out what happened at the villa after you left....'

'How can you?' Victoria was concerned. 'They will shoot you.'

Giorgio smiled. 'I'm not going anywhere near the villa, don't worry.'

'And Julio?' The young woman was leaning forward urgently in her seat. 'Where is he going?'

'Don't worry, Chiara, he's coming with me. He'll be OK.'

Giorgio nodded and was gone, and Victoria turned to look properly for the first time at her rescuer. This then, was Chiara, James's sweetheart, the girl who had turned his heart over, and his life. Giuseppe started the car and they moved away.

It was about ten minutes before Chiara spoke. 'You are James's sister?' she asked quietly.

'Yes, and you are Chiara. He told me about you.'

As Victoria felt Chiara's full gaze, she suddenly realized that Chiara was everything James had said. Although it was dark, she could see Chiara was a most beautiful woman.

'You were there,' Chiara said. 'What happened? Is James dead?'

Tears filled Victoria's eyes. 'I don't know. We were all trying to get away and James made us go, he said he would hold them up.' She stopped for a moment. 'There were lots of them,' she added hesitantly. 'I don't see how he could have escaped.'

Chiara nodded. 'I see,' was all she said. Guy met Victoria's eyes. His expression was anguished, but he turned back without a word.

Once again there was silence as the car jolted along, and Victoria sensed that Chiara was holding back her tears. Eventually, however, she spoke again. 'Try and rest, Victoria. See, Guiditta is already asleep.

We must get you as far as we can tonight, right out of the mountains if we can. Tomorrow the area will be crawling with Boche looking for you. Remember it is curfew, no cars allowed, but this is a very quiet area, so we should be alright. If we are stopped, leave the talking to Giuseppe. The story is that we are taking your mother, who is Guiditta by the way, to a doctor because her leg has not set properly.' Just who Guy was supposed to be, she did not explain.

'OK.' Victoria tried to settle down, but her thoughts were chaotic. *How many people are risking their lives tonight to save us? It all seems to be organized by Giorgio, but he had said he was not a partisan.... Does Chiara feel about James the way he had felt about her? Is it possible James is still alive?*

The car rattled on into the darkness.

CHAPTER FOURTEEN

Guy staggered to the side of the road and swung the heavy back pack to the ground. He was exhausted and sweating, and he bent and stretched several times, trying to get some feeling back into his painful shoulder muscles. Eventually, he took out his water bottle from a side pocket of the heavy pack, and took a deep draft before replacing it and sitting down on a convenient flat rock. When he had seen the rock out of the corner of his eye, he had known this could be a good spot to take a break. Ten minutes he told himself, ten minutes to unburden himself of the heavy pack, take a leak and a breather.

Only eleven o'clock and the sun was already high, and the valley spread out before him like a beautiful invitation in a tourist guide. *This must be some wonderful country when there isn't a war on....*

He screwed up his eyes against the sun, trying to ascertain the line of his journey, the way back to the Allied lines, which involved this detour around the area still occupied by the German army. He had hoped to spot some distant sign of activity, but could see nothing. That meant that Julio's directions were correct, he reasoned, at least so far. It was hard to imagine the mighty battles which were raging not so far away, perhaps even as near as the next valley.

He got out Julio's local map and examined the marked route again. It was pretty obvious from here, although he couldn't see the track itself, bordered as it was by thick bushes and undergrowth. But he could see in the distance the place where it joined the road, hardly a main road by the look of it, but a road which would no doubt need to be defended and fought over. The trouble was he didn't know whether that road, his immediate destination, had already been taken by the Allies or was still under German control. Well, another couple hours and he'd find out, that was for sure.

He looked back the way he had come. It was only a few hours since he had said goodbye to Victoria and Guiditta, who were to remain at the remote farmhouse where Giorgio had said they would be safe. His face clouded as he pondered that fact. How far could you trust a man like Giorgio? True, he had much to thank him for, he had undoubtedly gotten them away safely from the villa and had risked his life and those of his people in the process, but where did his allegiance lie? No one knew. Giorgio seemed to have many faces and many allegiances, and who were 'his people' anyway? What did that actually mean? He had heard the phrase often, 'oh – he's one of Giorgio's people....' Was he some sort of king who demanded loyalty like that? And why?

Guy still could not shake off the intense feeling of loss he had experienced when he said goodbye to Victoria. It had been so fast, everyone still tired and on edge after the events of the night before, but there could be no delay. The one thing he knew was that he had to get the contents of the back pack to HQ without delay. She had smiled that slow tremulous half smile in spite of everything, the smile that told him she was clinging to hope; hope for James, whatever the evidence.

They had embraced briefly, and he had said something about their next meeting being in New York, as it was not likely he would be coming back to Italy. He had said 'I'll come to see your parents...' and she had said, 'Yes please, they would like that. Keep safe.' And then he had gone, as fast as he could, under that compulsion to get away, away from her eyes, away from the look which said, 'How could you let this happen to my brother...?'

What would that be like? Trying to explain to James's parents that he had been shot down while the others all got away...? Couldn't think about it now ... not now.

Guy's thoughts wandered back to Giorgio, and then to his own boyhood experiences of the so-called Mob at home. In the run down area of Brooklyn where he had been brought up, it had been a way of life to make sure you kept on the right side of certain people. He had never been entirely certain who these people were, but sure as hell his Dad knew. An image of his father rose in his mind and suddenly he could almost smell him, the reek of his unwashed lumberjack shirt and old cotton pants, as he propped up the corner by Lannigan's Irish bar, available and ready to take the illegal bets which he passed on to someone called Joey, someone who was a daily part of life but who Guy had never seen, a ghostly provider of the little money which kept his small family at a subsistence level. A few times his Dad had trusted Guy to run to the little house behind Lannigan's with an envelope, which he had to give to the lady who opened the door, saying, 'This is for Joey, please, from my Dad.' The lady had never said a word, but had just taken the envelope with a disapproving tight-lipped frown, closing the door quickly.

The slight smile which the memory brought to Guy now was a bitter one. He recalled his poor, worn-out mother complaining about it, and receiving a swift slap for her pains. He knew by now that his Dad had been what was known as a 'bookie's runner' as well as a drunk, of course, and the knowledge that at seven years old his father had used Guy in illegal betting only served to deepen the contempt in which he had always held his father.

Rather different to James, he thought. James was never far from his thoughts. James and Victoria's father was Clancy Sullivan, a pillar of society, a very well respected Irishman who had started with nothing and had built up a huge restaurant and catering business by dint of his own, and his lovely wife's efforts. James and Victoria had been educated and brought up in circumstances very different to his own. And yet ... and yet.... There had been that thing about the family, that connection with the Mob. Victoria's real family ... her birth mother had been married to Paolo Vetti, and Paolo's uncle Vittorio had left Victoria the villa. James had explained it all to him, how it had been his fault, and how his family had nothing to do with it, but even so.... The tentacles of the Mob seemed to stretch far and wide, across oceans and into people's lives ... even when there was a war on.

And what about Victoria now? Guy found thinking about her gave him a feeling of absolute desperation. How could she have come to mean so much to him so quickly? He didn't really know her at all. But still she had invaded his life to such an extent that he would undoubtedly do something stupid if he allowed himself to speculate on the future. What would she do when the war ended? Go home, of course, home to the lovely old brownstone house in New York, home to the protective parents and the moneyed lifestyle....

Guy sighed. He knew that if and when he ever got back to New York he would have to keep his promise, go and see those same parents, talk to them about James. He stood and picked up the huge back pack. *Forget it, if you ever do see Victoria again, she won't be interested in a GI who comes from the place you do, someone who couldn't even keep her brother safe.*

He got painfully to his feet. In the meantime, he had a pack to deliver.

Victoria stared at Chiara, who was sitting in the garden slicing beans into a white bowl. The beans were the first of the season, and it had taken much husbandry and detailed care to be able to harvest them so early. Since they had been at the old farmhouse, Victoria had learned a lot more about producing food from the land, and under Guiditta's tutelage she had even managed to produce some half decent bread, once Giorgio had ensured they had flour. They were certainly not well fed, but they were surviving in this place of relative safety, away from the fierce fighting which was going on in the valleys below, and which they heard of, second and third hand, without really understanding what was going on. At least they were surviving, Victoria thought, and Chiara was surviving with them; pale and reticent, but still here.

Victoria studied her profile. Although Chiara was dark haired like Julio, her skin was fine, almost milky, a fragile contrast to the deep long-lashed chocolate eyes which now looked up and caught Victoria's gaze. She smiled, and it was breathtaking. Victoria understood, as she did every time she saw that smile, how James had been ensnared completely.

'What are you thinking?' Chiara's question came gently, kindly, although of course, she knew the answer.

'Oh … just….' What had she been thinking of? The same things which had boiled and simmered in her mind since that awful time, almost six weeks ago, when…. No! She would not, this time she would not mention his name. She would not have Chiara in tears again, not today….

'I was wondering if we shall see Giorgio soon…?'

'I doubt it. He has many things to do, people to see. The times are changing so fast and he has to keep up, he has many interests.'

'Do you think so? That times are changing fast, I mean? It seems to me to be dragging on forever, this awful war, we have been waiting for the Allies for so long.'

'But they are making progress now, at long last.' Chiara attempted to console her.

'Do you really think so?' Victoria was dismissive. 'All we hear about is casualties, so many … so many …. Americans, British, Polish, French…. I think Julio said there were some Tunisians, as well as Italians.' She stopped. 'All fighting, all being killed … and in France, nothing seems to be happening. My God! When is it going to be over?'

She did not often give way to such thoughts, and Chiara understood her distress. She too had similar thoughts, but it did no good to voice them. Instead, she tried to change the subject.

'I wonder if Guy got through alright.'

Victoria gave her a look of anguish, and began to cry softly.

'Oh, Vicki, Vicki....' Chiara put down the beans and came over to her. She put her arms around Victoria and held her close. 'Don't cry, Vicki, I know it's awful, but he's a strong man and …. I think … oh my dear, I think you have feelings for him, don't you? Such a good man. You love him don't you? Like I loved James?'

Victoria wiped her eyes. 'I thought so … at one time I thought so, but I didn't know if he felt the same, and when he left it was so awful, he seemed so cold....'

'He was suffering, Vicki, suffering like you and I … because of James.'

Here we are again. Even when I decide his name will not be mentioned, it always comes back to this. We shall never get over this, not Chiara, not me, and not Guy....

Aloud she said, 'He never said much but I know he and James had become very close.'

Chiara nodded quietly. 'And of course, he will be feeling very guilty.'

'Guilty?' Victoria was surprised. 'Why should he feel guilty?'

'I didn't say he *should,* of course, he has nothing to feel guilty about, but he will. Think about it – two soldiers who know each other well, they go on a mission together. One is killed, one survives. Of course the survivor feels guilty, even though it isn't his fault.'

'Do you really think Guy will be thinking like that?'

'Of course, it's only natural. Even if he got the information back to HQ and was given a medal for it, you can't alter the fact that he lived and his friend died. Especially because James....' Chiara's voice faltered. 'James saved us all by what he did. Guy will never forget that, and neither will I or Julio....'

Oh God, is that true? Does Guy really feel guilty because he survived? Of course it's true. If I feel guilty then Guy will too, although he only did exactly what he should and was as strong and brave as anyone. He followed orders and got the job done, whereas I ... I ... if only I could have kept Fleischer occupied....

'Guy was brave, and did what he had to do,' she whispered gently. 'If anyone has any guilt it is me. If I could have handled Fleischer better, perhaps we could have all gotten away –'

'No!' Chiara said firmly. 'It was no one's fault. Not yours, not Guy's, and not James's. You'll be telling me next that it was Guiditta's fault, because she shouldn't have shot Fleischer. These things happen ... it is the war ... the bloody war....'

Victoria nodded dumbly, she knew it was true, but it didn't make her feel any better.

'There is something you should know.' Chiara spoke softly. 'I am not sure I should tell you, but you will know soon anyway. I am expecting a child.' She smiled her wondrous smile. 'James's child.'

Victoria could hardly believe it. 'Oh? Are you sure?' She looked around as if for help to understand. 'I ... I don't know what to say....'

'I know,' Chiara soothed. 'It takes a while to get used to the idea. I am not married, and I know you are shocked, and you are probably disappointed in me, but it is a fact. I hope you will not feel too badly about me...?'

Their eyes met and suddenly they both began to smile and then to laugh together, and for some reason Victoria began to feel better at last.

Guy kept low, the back pack slowed him down and was not only heavy but cumbersome. Nevertheless, he made halting progress through the undergrowth alongside the road. He was bent double, picking his way, ears straining for the soft, menacing "pop" which would mean he had trodden on an S-mine left by the retreating Germans. He had no wish to be skewered by hundreds of steel bolts.

Rounding a slight bend, he suddenly heard a noise in the undergrowth ahead. Germans? He retreated slightly, aware he could be shot at any moment. His mouth was dry and he tried to blend into the hedgerow. Then there slowly emerged a US sergeant crawling through the undergrowth on his hands and knees, and Guy realized with exhilaration that at long last he had reached Allied lines. Which one, and exactly where, was only a vague idea. It took a few tense moments to identify himself, during which the sergeant attempted to hide his irritation under his professional shell.

'OK soldier, carry on,' he said curtly. 'About 6 miles to HQ, but you'll find a chow wagon about 2 miles back. Tell them Sergeant Shaunessy said to feed you.'

'Thanks, Sergeant.' He had made it! Back behind US lines and not only alive, but in one piece. The euphoria was short-lived. There was the sudden repeated whine of mortars and as Guy threw himself flat, he felt the earth heave beneath him as they hit. The sky fell in and earth dropped like rain around him. The dirt was dry and gritty in his mouth. Was this it? He struggled to his knees.

'You OK?'

He became aware of the sergeant bending over him, and nodded. 'Yes.'

'Get going then ... you're still far forward....'

'You're telling me!' Guy muttered, and crawled on his way.

For the next half mile or so Guy hardly stood up. The terrain was fairly open and he was afraid he would be an easy target if he didn't keep low. He kept close to the unkempt hedgerow, although it offered scant cover, and for most of the time was bent almost double as he made his slow way forward. Eventually he encountered the next US personnel, a group of engineers clearing mines from the sides of the road. They had strange apparatus strapped to their chests, and the long detector rods stretched out before them like antennae. They used the poles like divining rods, working very slowly and quietly, so that Guy felt he was caught up in a slow motion movie. The only sound was the sudden hum of one of the contraptions when it located a mine, and all movement stopped as the engineer in charge made it safe.

They were not at all interested in Guy, and waved him through quickly. He moved on, leaving them to their quiet concentration, and about two hundred yards further on he met up with the chow wagon and a young lieutenant from regional HQ he had met before. He was in charge of the wire section and was laying cables for the field telephones. He could not have been more than twenty, and his helmet was covered with twigs and leaves stuck into the helmet net.

'Hello, sir!' he said. He seemed genuinely pleased to see Guy, but then became slightly embarrassed. 'I feel like a woman with this greenery on my head.'

'I feel like a woman every day,' said a small grimy private who was unrolling cable. 'But I've had no luck yet.'

Guy laughed and recalled where he had met the lieutenant. 'You were on the ship when we came ashore at Anzio.'

The lieutenant nodded. 'Slightly more peaceful here just at the moment.'

'How are things going?' Guy asked, hungry for information.

'Search me,' the lieutenant said. He was, after all, not so relaxed as he appeared. 'How should I know? I got orders, that's all I know.'

He turned to the cable team and barked, 'Get a move on there,' as if to prove his point, before turning back to Guy. 'Sorry. I'd be OK if I could sleep for a couple years….'

'You're doing fine.' Guy's hand pressed the lieutenant's shoulder for a second. 'You're doing fine,' he repeated and carried on, moving with a little more confidence, knowing he was not far from the main line and that he could soon get rid of the damned back pack.

CHAPTER FIFTEEN
6th June 1944

She had been working in the garden all morning, and was desperate to know if there was news. As soon as Victoria heard the sound of the approaching car she began to run towards the farmhouse, knowing it could only be Giorgio. When she arrived at the farmhouse door he was already there, shaking hands with the old farmer and then with his wife. Chiara appeared from the kitchen, and Giorgio spread out his arms with an expansive smile.

'Hello, cousin, you are looking better.' He hugged Victoria briefly and then turned to Chiara. 'How are you, Chiara?' He kissed her on both cheeks and took her face in his hands, examining her intently. He nodded as if in approval, and then said softly, 'Yes. You are alright, I think? It has been bad but you are surviving, as we all are.'

'Is Julio coming too?' she asked urgently.

'I'm sorry, but he has had to stay to take care of things in Rome. Let's go inside.' Giorgio led the way into the farmhouse kitchen, where Maria and Guiditta were already pouring out glasses of home-made cordial. 'That looks very welcoming!' He flung himself onto an old sofa and everyone crowded round him, anxious for news. Accepting a glass of cordial, he took a deep draft, and then looked at them with a beaming smile.

'Yes, I have news at last, lots of news. Please....' He gestured to Alfonso and Maria to sit down, and made room for Chiara on the sofa. 'Please....'

Victoria sat down at the kitchen table with Guiditta, Alfonso, and Maria. She felt as if the world had stopped for a moment. The air was heavy with expectation but she was apprehensive, and was not sure she wanted to hear the news after all. It had been too long in coming … and perhaps…. She tried to read Giorgio's expression.

'Well first … they've gone,' Giorgio said flatly. 'The Germans. They have gone, from Rome, from the villa….' He tried to continue but could not because Victoria and Guiditta were shrieking, holding Alfonso and Maria and dancing them around the small kitchen. Chiara seized Giorgio and kissed him and then they all kissed him, again and again. Alfonso went over to the old corner cupboard and took out a green bottle.

'Only local wine and it's the last,' he said, 'but saved for this day. Sorry I have no brandy….'

Everyone finished up the cordial quickly so he could pour a measure of wine into their glasses, including Giorgio, who laughed and said, 'Yes, it is exciting when you hear it at first. You should have been in Rome yesterday … but I must tell you from the beginning. It was a few days ago that Kesselring ordered all the German units to break contact and withdraw. Of course, it was not generally known at the time, but I knew quite quickly, because –'

'You had your spies in there,' Chiara interrupted, laughing. 'I expect Paolo was able to get word to you…?'

'No,' Giorgio said shortly. 'I'm afraid not. It is not all good news. Paolo is dead, I'm afraid.'

The room fell silent and Victoria thought of the small man working in the kitchen, who had given her a loaf of bread.

'I'm so sorry,' Chiara said in a small voice. 'I know Paolo had worked for you for a long time.'

'Yes. Long before the war, and his family were always employed by my family,' Giorgio answered. 'He died the day after you escaped, apparently. They suspected him of being involved in the burglary and the shooting of Oberst Fleischer.'

'But he wasn't!' Guiditta blurted.

'I know, but he was caught in the garden. He had just moved the trash bin so James and Guy could get down from the attic.'

'But how do you know that?' Even as she said it Victoria knew it was a silly question.

Giorgio chose not to answer. 'Anyway, as I said, the order was given by Kesselring and the next day he declared Rome to be an open city and they started moving out, the tenth and fourteenth armies. From what I have heard it was quite an orderly retreat, although I had been dreading something awful, like what happened in Naples only last autumn. But there was no demolition or anything like that, they just left.' He paused. 'I think they just wanted to go, they had no time for anything else.' He took a sip of wine and continued. 'It was strange, as if the whole city was waiting for something. When they had all gone it was very quiet, but no one came out in the streets, everyone was holding their breath. Then, in the early hours of the morning, the Allies dropped leaflets, thousands of them.' He reached in his breast pocket. 'I've brought one for you.'

He passed around the crumpled sheet of paper and Victoria was elated to see the name of General Alexander at the bottom.

'I urge all Romans to stand shoulder to shoulder to protect the city from destruction, and to

defeat our common enemies,' she read aloud. *'Citizens of Rome, this is not the time for demonstrations. Obey these directions and go on with your regular work. Rome is yours! Your job is to save the city, ours is to destroy the enemy.'*

'We woke up to those leaflets on the fourth,' Giorgio explained. 'We read them and waited. There were reports that some 5th Army units had reached the outskirts of Rome, and there was a bit of scattered German resistance there, but not much. Then yesterday the whole 5th Army arrived in the city and everyone came out at last and shouted and cheered. It was quite a party ... everyone went mad ... it went on and on all day and into the night.' Giorgio shook his head, smiling at the thought of it. He shrugged. 'But the Americans hardly stopped; they just marched through the city and went north to follow the Germans. Only a few stayed in Rome.'

'Like ... who?' Victoria ventured.

'No one we know.' Giorgio's tone was dismissive and Victoria suddenly realized how tired he was. Nevertheless, he grinned briefly and added, 'I know you want news of your friend Guy, but I have heard nothing. Nothing at all. I did ask.' He hesitated and then said quietly, 'No news of your brother either, several people have reported he was killed, but no one knows what happened to his body. It just disappeared along with the Germans. So did Fleischer's apparently; perhaps the Germans took the dead with them, Paolo as well.'

Victoria sat down, deflated. *Oh my poor mother and dada, what can I tell them?*

'Also, there is a lot of work going on at the Ardeatine caves,' Giorgio continued. 'They are recovering the bodies already and they are being identified. There are many grieving families in Rome, as well as celebrations.'

There seemed nothing to say. Guiditta picked up the green bottle from the table and held it up. There was a small amount left which she carefully poured into Giorgio's glass. 'And the villa?' she asked. 'Have you been there?'

'Yes, I have just come from there. Most of the ... mess ... has been cleared away now and the place isn't too bad at all. In fact it's rather busy –'

'Busy? Who is there?' Victoria was startled.

'You'd better come and look. The Americans have taken it as a field hospital ... there are so many injured, and they are sending them back south to repatriate them to the USA. But some are not well enough to travel and so they asked if they could use the villa as a temporary measure.'

'They asked who?'

'Well ... me....'

Victoria bridled. 'Why did they ask you? It isn't your villa,'

'I know. They asked me because people directed them to me. I told them it was my cousin's villa and I'd have to ask you, but in the meantime....'

'What?'

'I thought you wouldn't mind. In fact, I told them I'm sure you wouldn't mind.'

'You had no right –'

'For goodness' sake, cousin!' Giorgio got to his feet. 'There was a queue of men bleeding to death at the door! Should I have sent them away?'

'Of course not! I'm sorry ... of course not. I just wondered why ... why....' *they got in touch with you,* she thought lamely. But of course, it all made sense, it was what always happened, what was happening all over Italy as the Allies moved north. As they captured a town or even a village, the Americans would ask, 'Who can we do business with here?' They wanted just to lay down some ground rules and move on.

The answer was always the local name which came quickly to the tongue, the local man who had always been in charge of things, and he would be summoned and put in charge again (if he wasn't already the mayor), and so the country was gradually turned over to the Mafia, or the Amici, as they preferred to be known.

Victoria sighed, and Giorgio said, 'I don't think it will be for long, a matter of months perhaps.'

Victoria nodded, feeling a little ashamed of her reticence. She turned to Alfonso and Maria. 'We shall not be a burden on you any longer. You have been so good to care for us all this time, but we can go home now, Guiditta and me.' She turned to Giorgio. 'Are you intending to go back today? You must be exhausted.'

He smiled. 'I am, but if you can spare a little food, I'll have that and a couple hours sleep. Then we can go back together, later this afternoon. We'll be at the villa before nightfall.'

While Giorgio slept in Alfonso's bed, Victoria took him and Maria aside and thanked them profusely for their help. She was very conscious of the fact that without it they would have been in fear of their lives. Returning to the kitchen, she found Guiditta sobbing at the table. She sat down beside her but said nothing, knowing her friend must be as sick at heart as she was.

Guiditta raised a tear-stained face. 'That poor man. It wasn't his fault and he's dead, and James, too. It's all my fault, I should not have shot Fleischer....'

'No,' Victoria said gently. 'It's my fault.' She stopped. It was hard to say the words. 'If I had done my job properly ... kept Fleischer entertained ... none of it would have happened.'

'But he was going to rape you!' Guiditta sobbed. 'I couldn't let that happen.'

'I know. I know. It wasn't your fault ....' Victoria took her hand. 'Be calm now, and listen to me. I should never have let things get to that situation. If I had said yes to Fleischer right away, none of it would have happened. It would have been a small sacrifice, and James and Paolo would both perhaps still be alive –'

'But you couldn't have done that!' Guiditta was genuinely shocked.

'But I should have!' Victoria's tone was bitter. 'Do you think my virginity is worth a man's life? The lives of two men? Believe me; I'd throw it away a dozen times if I thought I could bring my brother back.'

'It's still my fault,' Guiditta protested. 'I fired the shot and woke them all up –'

Giorgio's voice broke in. 'It's nobody's fault, so stop this conversation now!' He was standing in the doorway. 'Nobody's fault,' he repeated. He came over, sat beside Guiditta and took her hand. 'It's the war,' he explained. 'Just the bloody war.' He turned to Victoria. 'But you are right, cousin, you should have done what Fleischer asked. In wartime only one thing is important and that is survival. You do what you have to do. So many people are making compromises, large and small, to make sure we win this war and put an end to the whole mad business. I am sorry if that makes you feel worse,' he added, seeing Victoria's distraught face, 'but the same rule still applies. We have no time for recrimination, no time to feel sorry for ourselves or anyone else.' He took Victoria by the shoulders and shook her gently. 'We are here, cousin, and we are alive. We fight on and don't look back. The time to do that is when we are old and grey and can see things in perspective. For now ... we fight on.'

'May I come too?' Chiara had been listening.

'Of course,' Victoria said. 'We shall all fight on together.'

CHAPTER SIXTEEN

The villa looked different. German vehicles had been replaced by American troop carriers, ambulances and trucks, both on the main road and along the drive to the villa. The large front lawns were dotted with marquees and tents, temporary field dressing stations, and all the general paraphernalia of an army on the move. On the whole it looked fairly well ordered, although there was a short queue of ambulances waiting to unload their patients near the villa entrance, and Victoria watched in distress as harassed nurses and stretcher carriers bent over their bloody burdens.

They had been stopped at the entrance to the drive by an armed US sentry, who took an age to obtain permission for them to proceed to the villa. When they got there, another sentry attempted to turn them away again.

Giorgio turned to Chiara. 'You wait in the car. I don't want you exposed to all this … chaos.'

Chiara nodded. Giorgio had explained that he had made arrangements for her to go back to teaching at the small school on the outskirts of the city, the job she had held until the school had closed. Now, as he got out of the car, Victoria breathed, 'Does he know?'

'No,' Chiara said. 'I'll tell him when I have to, but it is a good idea for me to go back to work. I shall need the money and I might as well work while I can.'

Victoria nodded. 'OK, I can see that, but if you have any problem, you know where we are.'

Chiara smiled her thanks, and opened the car window. Outside, Giorgio was getting angry.

'I am here with the owner of this building!' he explained for the tenth time. 'Please let Major Simons know I am here. He is expecting us!'

Eventually, they were allowed into the reception hall where the whole procedure had to be repeated again, but after about fifteen minutes they were at last led towards the drawing room. The room which had been great uncle Vittorio's drawing room – and Fleischer's office.

Victoria drew in her breath as they entered the room, she could feel herself trembling. But it was only an army office again, with extra filing cabinets and the big desk still in the same place. A tired-looking US officer was in the seat where Fleischer had sat.

He got up and extended a hand to Giorgio. 'Good to see you again, Mr. Vetti.' The two men shook hands and the Major added, 'I see you have been successful.'

He gave Victoria a smile and she suddenly saw him as Italians must see him, he looked so very ... American. She felt a thrill of joy, and wanted to weep.

'Yes, this is my cousin, Miss Vetti,' said Giorgio, gesturing as if he had just produced her from a hat. 'The owner of this villa.' He turned to Guiditta. 'And this is Guiditta Alvaro. She has worked in this building for over thirty years, and knows more about it than almost anyone.'

Major Simons smiled again. 'It's good to meet you at last. Miss Vetti. And you too, Signora Alvaro.' He shook hands with them both. 'Thank you for allowing us to use this lovely building for a while. We do not expect to need it for long.'

'You are welcome, Major,' Victoria said. 'Do you have any idea how long you will need to be here?'

'No longer than we can possibly help, that's for sure,' he responded. 'About two months would be my best guess. We have a fast repatriation policy for our wounded, and planes leave every day from the south. We only keep patients until they are ready to travel.' He rose. 'Perhaps you would both like to see exactly what we are doing here? I could give you a quick tour.'

'Thank you,' said Victoria, and she and Guiditta followed the Major towards the wide staircase.

By the time the tour was finished, Victoria was barely able to speak. She had known something of the horrors of war, but this was different. Only the worst cases had been brought inside the building, where the largest bedrooms, previously used to house the German staff and officers, were now converted to small wards. The injured men lay in various stages of consciousness, some as if already dead, their pallor adding to that effect, while others were not only awake, but talkative and good humored. They had been pleased to see the visitors, especially when they learned Victoria was from the USA.

'Most of the patients are in the marquees on the front lawns,' Major Simons informed them as they descended the staircase. 'Almost all we do is directed towards the prevention of infection. The wounds are varied and need treatments from simple closure and suturing to complete excision of tissue which has been devitalized ... and of course, amputation if necessary.'

Victoria nodded. 'But I suppose some treatment is done immediately, I mean at the front...?'

'Not if we can help it.' Major Simons gave a smile. 'We don't let some half-trained medic loose on our men. They are allowed to try to stop blood flow and get the patient to the nearest dressing station, that's all.'

He continued as they re-entered the office. 'In the past too many men died from wounds which had been closed too quickly, before they were properly cleaned and disinfected. Our main aim is to get them to expert help fast. And that is why we have these field dressing stations and temporary hospitals. Everyone here is top class in their field, and fresh blood is flown in daily, although we use plasma where we can. We aim not to lose anyone.'

'But of course,' Victoria said. 'I am wondering if there is any way I can help?'

'Are you a qualified nurse?'

'No,' she said. 'At my college in Switzerland we had very basic nursing training, mainly to equip us for looking after our future families. But I could do an orderly's job, giving out drinks, keeping them cheerful, writing letters home, fetching bedpans....'

'And emptying them?' the Major quizzed.

'And emptying them,' Victoria said firmly. 'No problem.'

'In that case you start tomorrow. We have some volunteers here already, the Romans seem very willing to help us and our wounded, but you have a big advantage over most of them.'

'Oh? What is that?'

'You speak their language and understand what makes them tick ... and you speak ours too.'

Victoria smiled as Guiditta volunteered, 'Is there something I can do?'

It was Giorgio who answered. 'No, Guiditta, your leg is not quite well yet, we don't want to try it too much, you can look after yourself and Vicki.'

Victoria turned to the Major. 'Do you know if the cottage in the garden is being used? We have been living there until recently ... when the Germans were here.'

'I'll find out,' said the Major, picking up the telephone.

It took very little time for Victoria and Guiditta to settle back into the cottage. They were able to gather their things together from the attic quite quickly, and were astonished when a kitchen orderly approached them as they left the villa.

'Miss Vetti?' he asked, smiling. 'I have some food packs here for you to take to the cottage, Major Simons instructions. I'll bring them along for you as you have enough to carry already. When you have seen what there is you can let me know if you will need anything else.'

Victoria translated his words for Guiditta, and laughed as the old lady looked across at her and winked heavily. Times had changed indeed.

The following weeks passed quickly in a flurry of hard work, confusion and sheer exhaustion. Major Simons had been right, the Italian volunteers were seeking clear directions which they could follow, and because of her language skills Victoria found herself pivotal to the organization of the villa.

Once she understood what was required, (and Major Simons was nothing if not succinct) she was able to see what was needed and make it happen. Within the first couple weeks his operating systems were clearly established, and the whole volunteer workforce took over all the background tasks required for efficient operation. The medical and nursing staff, a little apprehensive at first, were delighted to be able to spend more time on real patient care and gladly cooperated and advised when Victoria needed it, and then left it all to her.

Although she had started out feeding and washing patients and emptying bedpans, Victoria soon became the focal point where the others came for instructions when they came on shift. She became the unofficial administrator. In the midst of this strenuous work, she was aware of a deep sense of satisfaction; she was doing something useful at last, something which made a difference. When she reached the cottage tired out after her shift, Guiditta would be there with a sympathetic word and a hot meal, and they settled back into the easy relationship they had begun to develop before the Germans invaded their lives.

They saw nothing of Giorgio, but after six weeks Victoria received a letter from Chiara. She wrote in hastily scrawled Italian from Carlo's old farmhouse and hoped they were alright. She had met up with Julio again, and he was fine too. Then the letter continued, more hesitantly:

'I had seen nothing of Giorgio until last week, but I knew he would arrive when Julio came home, so then I got both of them together and told them about the baby. You can imagine? They were both very angry with me but Giorgio was the worst. After a lot

of shouting they sent me to bed and Giorgio said they would 'deal with me' in the morning. I was not surprised because it was what I had expected, but next morning they had calmed down. Julio said they had talked about it and would help me as much as they could. He said 'After all, it is not so bad, nobody's died.' And then I got very angry at last and I shouted at them. I said, 'Yes, they have! The baby's father has died! Have you forgotten?' Then they looked really shocked and we all ended up hugging each other for comfort and they said they would never forget James and what had happened.'

The letter continued with greetings from them all, and from Alfonso and Maria, and Chiara promised she would come to visit them as soon as it was possible. Victoria could not help but speculate about the coming child, certainly it would have love from Chiara and her family (*a Mafia family!* said the voice in her head), but this was James's child, her own niece or nephew, and surely her beloved parents in New York would have, and should have, a view about its future. The little voice whispered, *but you are not a real blood relative,* but then countered with, *but your parents are, this is their grandchild we are talking about.*

Victoria had already written lengthy epistles to her parents, because as soon as she had settled back into the cottage, Major Simons had allowed her to send letters via the US Army mail. The first reply came quickly, and she wept copiously as she read her mother's brave words, words of comfort and love, all the more endearing because they hid a depth of anguish Victoria could only guess at. *'We knew about James already,'* her mother had written. *'The Army sent a telegram and then someone came to see us, but they seemed to know no details, and your letter helped us to understand what had happened. I'm so glad you saw him, darling, so very glad....'*

Victoria sighed. How could she ever tell her mother what really happened? All of it? After all, James *was* their own child, *a blood relative,* as Giorgio would say.

That evening over their simple meal, she brought up the subject of the letters with Guiditta, showing her the one from Chiara, and then translating her mother's into Italian. Guiditta listened intently, and then said: 'I know what you are thinking. You didn't tell her, did you? About the baby?'

Victoria hesitated, before admitting, 'No.'

'Why not?'

'It didn't seem right when I first wrote. I thought they had enough to contend with, hearing about James....'

'And are you going to tell them now?'

'I'm thinking about it. Well yes, I know they have a right to know, but I'm not sure....'

'Not sure of what?'

'Well, I don't know how they will react. They will be happy about it, of course, at least I think so, but it could become so complicated. What if they want to have the baby and give it a home? That's the sort of people they are, after all they took me in and brought me up as their own. They are the grandparents, after all.'

'And what about Chiara? She's the mother; she has most rights, surely?'

'Yes, of course she has, that's what makes it difficult. I think she will want to bring up this baby on her own....'

'Are you sure of that? It is a very great shame in Italy to bring a child into the world when you are not married. I'm not surprised Giorgio and Julio were so angry. I suspect Giorgio has already found a likely young man to marry her quickly, before everyone knows about it –'

'What?' Victoria was shocked. 'He wouldn't do that, would he?'

'Of course he would! He would be doing her a favor.' Guiditta leaned forward across the table. 'Victoria, this pregnancy will change Chiara's life forever. She will not be able to live normally and openly ever again. This is Italy, not New York. Things are different here, Chiara is lucky not to have been thrown out onto the streets....'

'Guiditta! How can you say such things? I thought you would understand –'

'Of course I understand,' Guiditta snapped. 'I am a woman who has seen this kind of thing many times, and I am sympathetic. But this is a man's world and I am telling you how it is, that's all. I know what will happen to her unless Giorgio can get someone to take her.'

Get someone to take her! That wonderful young woman, so beautiful and kind, the girl James adored....

Victoria rose, and began to clear the plates. 'I think you are probably right,' she said. 'Thank you, Guiditta; I know what I must do. I must ask Chiara if she would like to come home with me when I go back to New York. The baby will probably be here then, and they will both be very welcome there.'

'Ha! That might not be so easy. There are rules about such things you know. And you would have to ask your parents first.'

Victoria turned, her face set and her voice firm. 'No I do not. I am quite sure what their answer would be.'

Whether Victoria was sure or not, she lost no time in writing again to her parents. This time she informed them in the gentlest and most loving terms about James and his love for Chiara. She described Chiara, and explained her role in the rescue from the villa on that dreadful night, her kindness since then, and her grief for James. Then she disclosed the existence of the child, and asked if she might offer Chiara and the child a place with the family in New York.

She explained this was her own idea, but that she thought it a good one, as life for an unmarried mother in Italy was very hard. It was not easy in the US, she knew that, but the hardship was of a different kind and degree, and she reiterated that what Chiara and the child needed most was a loving home. It was after eleven o'clock when she finished the letter, and she went to bed that night with anxious thoughts, not so much about her parents' reaction but as to whether she was doing the right thing for Chiara. She tossed fitfully before she suddenly realized it was not really her responsibility. It was up to Chiara to decide. If she said yes, that would be wonderful, but if she said no, then that was alright too.

Next morning, Victoria picked up the letter after a quick breakfast and walked to the villa as usual, but when she got to the reception area to hand it in, the sergeant on duty smiled enthusiastically and said, 'Oh, Miss Vetti, there's one for you here….'

He held out the letter, it was grubby and crumpled, and as soon as she saw the handwriting Victoria felt a sudden panic. She did not know the writing but it could only be from Guy … it had come through Army mail but not the normal USA pack. As she raced upstairs to her work desk she stared at it fixedly, a firm sloping hand, to *Miss Victoria Sullivan (Vetti)* and the villa address. It could only be from Guy….

There were two volunteers already waiting at the desk, and Victoria got them organized for their shifts before she sat down and opened the letter. As she pulled the two thin sheets open, she realized her hands were trembling. There was an address at the top which had been blacked out by the censor, but the date was six days ago, and the rest of the letter was clear of censorship.

Dear Victoria,

It seems an age since we said goodbye at Alfonso and Maria's house, and let me first send greetings to them and you and Guiditta, and Giorgio if he is around. I am sending this to the villa, as when I enquired I found out it was being used as a field hospital, and I have the idea you will be there by now. Is Chiara with you and have you seen Julio again? I shall never forget their help that awful night and I'm sure you feel the same. It took me three days to get back to my unit, and whether the stuff I got out was needed or helpful I'll never know. I was able to tell them about James and they said they would let your parents know. I am still on the move, don't know exactly where I'm going but it's not too hard to make a wild guess.

By now you will have all the news about the Normandy invasion, who would have thought that when we were doing all that stuff at the villa it was all planned and ready to go? I have not heard much about what happened in Italy after I left. As soon as the Allies were in France, the news networks concentrated on nothing else but that.

It is hard to know what to say, I think of you and Guiditta every day and of James. I suppose no matter how much we dwell on it, we just carry on and put one foot in front of the other and hope that one day it gets us to the point we can perhaps meet again, probably in New York, where we shall both be heading when all this is over. I look forward to that day. I shall certainly go to see your parents when I get home if you think that would help, even in a small way. I know you can't answer this letter but if I can I'll try to get a firm address to you and we can perhaps exchange news?

Take great care of yourself and give Guiditta a big kiss from me,

Love, Guy.

Victoria read the letter through twice before she relaxed a little. He was alive, and that was all that mattered. He must be in France on his way to one of the various fronts which seemed to be opening there. '*We can perhaps meet again, probably in New York,*' he had written. She tried to imagine it, tried to put him at the front door of her parents' big brownstone house, but the image flickered and would not stay. '*And give Guiditta a big kiss from me,*' but not one for her, no kisses at the bottom, a good letter, a very welcome letter, but not really warm, a bit formal perhaps?

Victoria put the pages back into the envelope. Then she suddenly clutched the letter to her chest and burst into tears, tears of sadness and relief. Minutes later the duty nurse found her there, still sobbing, and made her a cup of coffee.

CHAPTER SEVENTEEN

It was mid-August, and in the heavy summer heat the field hospital was disbanding. All the patients who had been nursed in the big marquees on the lawn had long been sent south to be repatriated, and the villa looked almost back to normal, if you discounted the one or two ambulances and field trucks parked outside.

As she made her way from the cottage, Victoria decided not to wait for a reply from her parents before she approached Chiara with her plan.

Inside, there were only eight patients still remaining, and they were due for repatriation very soon. When Victoria remarked that they still seemed to be very ill, Major Simons agreed.

'Of course they are. They will not recover for months, perhaps years. They only have to be well enough to travel, that's all.'

'But it's such a long journey....'

'Yes, it is. But for them it will be no different to being here. They will be stretchered all the way to the plane, and the plane is specially fitted out to take them and care for them, with highly qualified staff all the way. It's done in stages too, not too much at once.' He laughed, it was clear Victoria was still concerned. 'Don't worry. We never lose anyone in transit, and you should see their faces when they know they are going home.'

'I suppose so.' Although Victoria was glad to know the villa would soon be hers again, she could not help but realize how much she was going to miss them all.

'There's something I wanted to ask you about,' Major Simons said. 'Have you a minute?'

They went into what he regarded as his office, and what Victoria still regarded as the drawing room. They sat down and Major Simons said, 'I wanted to thank you, officially I mean, not only for the loan of the villa but for all your help. You are a very good organizer, you have made our stay here much easier than it might have been.'

'It's been a pleasure, Major. I have enjoyed your being here.'

He regarded her fondly. 'Yes, I know you have, that is what has been so good about it. I wanted you to know that the Army might be able to repay your kindness, that is, if you wish it.'

'Oh?'

'Well, I know your home is in New York and you are intending to go back when you can. As a civilian it is still not easy to travel, but if you wanted to go fairly soon, you could hitch a lift on our Army flight. You could go back with our last patients, if you would like that. We repatriate from Naples and Foggia to Tunis first, and then on from there. A free trip home –who knows when you will be able to get back if you don't take the offer?'

'Really? I could really get a lift home?'

'Of course. I just have to do some paperwork for you.'

'Is it allowed?'

He laughed. 'It is if I say it is. After all, you are a United States citizen, you have provided us with a field hospital for nearly three months ... and you are now one of our well respected staff.'

Victoria laughed out loud. 'Oh what a wonderful surprise! When do I have to be ready?'

'Our last patients go home in two weeks' time. If you can be ready by then, we're in business.'

Victoria chose to wait until after she and Guiditta had eaten their evening meal before broaching the subject of Major Simons's amazing offer. She led Guiditta out to the small kitchen garden, where they still sat occasionally to enjoy the cooling air of early evening.

'I have something to tell you,' she began.

'Not another letter from Guy already?' Guiditta giggled, as she had several times when she thought of the "big kiss at the bottom" Guy had sent her.

'No, it's a bit too early to expect another letter yet.'

'You never know, sometimes they get held up and three come together....' Guiditta stopped when she saw Victoria's seriousness. 'Is it bad news?

'No, far from it, just a bit of a surprise. Major Simons has offered me a trip back to the States with the last of his patients, if I want it.'

Guiditta's mouth dropped open, her face registering complete horror. Victoria watched as she tried to rearrange her expression before she said, 'And do you? Want it?'

'It is not so much wanting it, I hadn't even considered it, but of course when he offered me the lift I realized it would be a great opportunity, one I can't really turn down. If I don't accept it, I will probably not get home for ages....'

Victoria stopped, then began again earnestly, 'Guiditta, it would be so good to see my parents, they have been having such a dreadful time ... hearing about James. I know it would help them to see me home safe.'

Guiditta nodded. 'Of course, of course. I understand, but what about the villa?'

'Well, of course I wouldn't be able to go if I didn't have you here to look after it for me. I shall leave you in charge, there is a great deal to do. The villa must be restored to its original condition, and only you know how to get that done. It will be difficult, but if anyone can do it you can, a little at a time. You will need to hire help of course, I will leave money for what you need, and your pay will go into the bank as usual. In future you will be needed to make sure everything is kept up properly, including the garden. I would like you to live there,' she continued, 'and become the housekeeper again, as you were for uncle Vittorio.'

She paused, watching as the idea flexed itself in Guiditta's mind. Victoria saw that she liked it.

'It will not be forever,' she said. 'When things settle down I shall certainly come back again, for a long visit.'

Guiditta nodded. 'I certainly would enjoy getting the old place back into shape, it has been dreadful watching the damage and the changes.' She smiled. 'I would have preferred if we did it together, but of course I know you must take the chance to be with your parents now. You need not worry about the villa, I know what to do.'

'I know that.' Victoria smiled her relief. 'I have one problem though, this has all happened so fast, we only have two weeks, and I must speak to Chiara quickly.'

'I see.' Guiditta obviously thought things were moving rather too fast. At length however, she said, 'Don't worry, I will contact one of Giorgio's people and get a message to Chiara.'

By now, Victoria was used to the underground system of communication via *"Giorgio's people"* but she still had no idea how it worked. When she asked, Guiditta simply said, 'I have a number to ring ... I can always contact Giorgio if I need to.'

It had always been thus, Victoria reminded herself with mild fury. *Why does everything always have to go by word of mouth and in such a circuitous way?* Of course, the answer was simple – so that Giorgio always knew exactly what was going on.

'I only want to see Chiara, and as quickly as possible,' she said briskly. 'There is no need for Giorgio to be involved.'

Guiditta looked dismayed. 'But surely ... surely you will not go back to America without saying goodbye to him?'

Now Victoria felt guilty. 'Well, no, of course not. I didn't think of it that way. But I don't want him putting pressure on Chiara to stay here, if she would rather come with me.'

Guiditta laughed. 'It is not a matter of what Chiara wants,' she said. 'What Giorgio decides, she will do. It is a matter of family.'

And what about my family? Victoria was about to remonstrate, but then she thought better of it. It was not Guiditta's fault and not her decision. She smiled and said simply, 'Let's see what happens.'

She did not have long to wait. Two days later Giorgio and Chiara both arrived, Giorgio driving a US Army jeep. *Where on earth has he gotten that from?* Victoria wondered, as she embraced them both and led them down to the cottage. It was a lovely morning and they sat out on the small terrace at the back, bordering the tiny vegetable plot.

They had hardly sat down when Giorgio went on the attack. 'I understand you both know about Chiara's disgrace,' he said, looking levelly at Victoria. 'It did not occur to you to get in touch with me. I was only told last week!'

Victoria was taken aback. 'It was not my news to tell, Giorgio. It was Chiara's business and I knew she would tell you when she felt it was right.'

'I wanted to tell Julio before anyone else,' Chiara offered lamely. Giorgio ignored her.

'Anyway, things move on,' Victoria said quickly. 'I have some news and I think it may help the situation.'

Giorgio glanced at her expectantly and she smiled at him. 'The Army has offered me a lift home.'

What?' Giorgio was not expecting that.'I can go back with the last patients from here.'

'But why?' He seemed stunned. 'Why would you want to go now, when you have just gotten the villa back?'

'Giorgio!' she responded sharply. 'Of course I want to see my parents as soon as I can! I have been waiting to get out of here for two years!' Seeing the consternation on his face, she added quickly, 'Anyway, it's an opportunity I can't miss for free flights, and in the circumstances I thought Chiara might want to come with me, that is, if they will allow it. There's probably some red tape –'

'What?' For once, Giorgio was lost for words.

'I realize this is something of a surprise,' Victoria continued. 'But I know you were unhappy about the child. My parents,' *the baby's grandparents*, 'will welcome the child and love it, because of James … and they will love Chiara too –'.

'What?' Giorgio was ready to explode. 'You think your parents can steal another baby away from my family?'

'What do you mean, another baby?'

'You!' Chiara said quickly. 'He means you, Victoria.'

'Me? What do you mean?'

'Yes, I mean you! I talk about you!' Giorgio was really angry. 'Your great uncle Vittorio, he was always good to me. Others say bad things about him because it is what they say about all of our family, and when he was in trouble in the States and your parents were killed, he had a dead nephew and a small baby to consider –'

'Yes, I know, I know the story.'

'You know what your parents have told you!' Giorgio was shouting now. 'They took advantage of his situation and took you from him! Yes! I know you will say they gave you a good life. Perhaps they did, but you belong to us. To us! Blood relatives!'

Victoria was too stunned to reply. She had, of course, always known about her birth and how she had survived as a tiny baby when her heavily pregnant mother was taken to hospital fatally injured in an explosion, part of the Mafia gang war raging at the time. The blast had killed her father too, and she had always understood that her great uncle Vittorio had begged Clancy and Anna Sullivan, close friends of his dead nephew Paolo, to take the tiny baby and give her a good life.

'It was not like that!' she said, realizing that no matter how it had seemed to her, she had no idea how it had seemed to Giorgio and his family. 'Great uncle Vittorio wanted me to stay in America. He said it was what my parents would have wanted –'

'Maybe it was, but it was not what we wanted! Uncle Vittorio used to talk to me when I was a boy, and tell me I had a cousin, the daughter of my dear friend Paolo, a lovely girl who lived in America, and that one day I might meet her. When he left you the villa and you arrived here, I thought you had come home at last....' He turned away, and his tone became bitter, full of disgust. 'But you only came for the villa didn't you? Not to meet your real family!'

'No Giorgio, it wasn't just for the villa. But we are not cousins ... not even near to being cousins.'

It was true. She understood that her great uncle Vittorio and Giorgio's grandfather had been brothers, but what on earth that meant she had no idea.

Giorgio was making a supreme effort to recover his composure, and Victoria realized that he was actually hurt by this encounter, not simply angry. He said briefly, 'No, we are not cousins, you are right, it is just a word I use. It is a distant relationship, of course, heaven knows what, but family is family, and we wanted to make you welcome.'

'And you did! You have! What I would have done without your help these last two years I'll never know.' Victoria caught hold of Giorgio's hand and pressed it. 'I know you are my family and I will always be proud of that, but you must understand that the Sullivans are good people, they loved me and cared for me all my life, and so of course I think of them as my parents. They *are* my parents.'

Giorgio held on to her hand a moment longer and Victoria thought, or did she imagine... a misting in his dark eyes? Surely not?

'Giorgio,' she said gently. 'The decision about Chiara's baby is hers to take. Not mine, or my parents', and not yours. It is only Chiara's.'

'Ha!' What he thought of that was obvious, but he said quietly, 'Chiara will have to think about this. I will leave you to it.' He left the terrace and walked back alongside the cottage and towards the villa.

Victoria looked at Guiditta and Chiara, who had both remained silent during this interchange. Neither of them met her eyes.

'What have I said that is so awful?' she asked. 'Is it such a terrible idea for the baby's grandparents to see it?'

'No, it isn't a terrible idea at all, in fact it is a nice idea,' said Chiara. 'But Victoria, you presented it as a *fait accompli*; as if it was the answer to everything … it is not.'

'You don't like the idea? Of coming to the US with me?'

'I certainly do not.' Chiara was emphatic. 'I would never travel that distance on a plane, several planes I expect, when I am pregnant, even if they would let me, which I'm sure they won't. And I will never leave my family and take my baby to strangers –'

'Strangers? They are James's parents, and we are talking about James's home!'

'Of course, that is how they are to you, but to me they are strangers, and my baby will not have James, only me! When I knew my darling James, it was here, all the short time I knew him he was here … not in America. He is still here, if they could only find his body….' Chiara began to cry, and Guiditta put her arms round her and soothed her gently.

Victoria felt the tears well up in her own eyes, they were tears of loss and of frustration too. How could she have gotten this so wrong?

'I'm sorry, Chiara, I wouldn't have said anything if Giorgio hadn't been so angry about it all. From what he said I thought he would be glad for you and the baby to go away and be looked after....'

'Oh, Victoria! You have everything wrong about Giorgio! Just because he was angry doesn't mean he doesn't love us. He will always look after us, no matter what. We are family, and so are you.' Chiara sighed. 'Surely you must understand by now without me having to spell it out!'

'Understand?' Victoria looked from one to the other. It was Guiditta who eventually spoke.

'You silly girl, have you still not realized? Giorgio is in love with you?'

CHAPTER EIGHTEEN

It took a moment for Guiditta's preposterous remark to sink in. Victoria began to smile, this was surely a joke? But they were not laughing, and it slowly dawned on Victoria that she had missed something here, something obvious to others but not to her. She had gotten it wrong. Again.

'I don't think so,' she said at last. 'He has never once given me any indication....' She stopped. 'Most of the time he is disagreeing with me about something or other.'

'Of course,' Chiara said, as if it was the most obvious thing in the world. 'He disagrees with you because he takes you seriously. Do you think he explains his thinking to me? Or Guiditta? No. He tells us what is to be done and we follow his advice. We do not argue with him and tell him he is wrong.'

'But that means you are ...' Victoria struggled for words, '... like slaves ... you have no minds of your own....'

Chiara did not take offence. Instead she laughed and said gently, 'Not at all, we listen to Giorgio because we know he is on our side, we know he will be there for us when we need him, like he was for you.'

'Is he always right then?'

Chiara laughed again. 'Of course not. Why are you always wanting to believe him to be a tyrant? If I really want to say something to him that I feel is important, I ask to speak to him and put my point of view, and he always listens.'

'Like he did about the baby, you mean?' Victoria said sarcastically.

'Yes. Exactly like he did about the baby, once he had calmed down. And, Victoria, he was not angry for himself, but for me. He thought I had spoiled my chances and he was probably right about that.'

'And so why? Why should you think he is in love with me? I cannot believe it.' Victoria felt alone, almost under attack, and certainly unlovable.

Guiditta, who had been pulling a few spring onions, seemed to understand. She came over and gave Victoria a motherly kiss. 'My dear, dear child, he loves you because he can't help himself. Like we all do, although of course, he is a man and so has to make *a song and dance* about it, isn't that the way you say it in English?'

'Yes, that's the way you say it.' Victoria smiled. 'But I don't think he's made much of a *song and dance* about it if I didn't even notice!'

'You didn't notice because you don't know him like we do,' Guiditta explained. 'I knew right way, the first time you met.'

'Really?'

'Yes! Believe me, I have been watching for years for Giorgio to find a nice girl, I wanted to see him married and with some *bambinos.* But he never seemed interested in anyone. When he met you at the cottage, I could see right away it was different. He never took his eyes off you.' Guiditta sighed. 'I can't imagine why you didn't notice.'

'But why didn't you say something?'

'Because I knew it could never come to anything, of course. Such different backgrounds and a different way of looking at things ... you are not right for each other.'

'Well, that's something we can agree on. We certainly are not!'

At that moment Giorgio walked out from the kitchen. He gave no inkling that he might have heard them discussing him, but simply announced, 'It can't be done. I have been talking to Major Simons, and he confirms he can take Victoria because of special circumstances, but he could never get permission for Chiara to go, even if she could get her documents in time.'

'Giorgio, I don't want to go,' Chiara said. 'I would not have agreed to it, not while I am pregnant, not even if it was possible.'

'I see.' He seemed to relax a little. 'At least someone is showing some common sense.'

'Giorgio, I was not trying to force anyone to do anything!' Victoria said. She tried to keep her tone light. 'When this blasted war is over, times will change. The baby will be here then, and perhaps Chiara can visit us in the US … just for a holiday, and the baby can meet his or her grandparents … and auntie?'

'Perhaps. Let's get the war over first. In the meantime, you are determined to go?'

'Yes, I think I must. For many reasons.'

Guiditta broke in. 'It's time to make some lunch so you can eat before you go. Thanks to the US army, we can offer you something edible. Chiara, come and help me, will you?'

They went into the tiny kitchen, leaving Giorgio and Victoria to survey the few rows of remaining onions in the small vegetable plot.

'I don't understand why it has to be now,' Giorgio said quietly. 'You could stay until the war is over, and be here when the baby is born.'

'I could, but Giorgio, I don't want to do that. All I can think of is that my poor mother and Dada are alone and are grieving for James. It would be such a comfort for them to have me there with them.'

'Of course, James was their blood child, am I correct? But you are not.'

'You are correct. James was their blood child, as you call it. I was adopted after Vittorio left.'

'He did not "leave," he was deported, wasn't he?'

'Yes, I believe he was.'

'And if you died, would the Sullivans grieve for you the same as for James?'

'I think so. Yes, they would.'

'So they were always good to you? Vittorio said they would be.'

'He was right, they loved me as their own.'

'Good. I am glad for that. Then please do not give them something else to grieve over. Do not go now, wait until the war ends –'

'But that might be years!'

'Not so long now, everyone says now the Allies are in France it will not be so long –'

'But I can't! I have a chance to go and I must!' Victoria was vehement.

'But the planes ... it is still wartime ... you might be shot down!'

Suddenly Victoria understood. It was as Chiara said, he was afraid for her.

'No Giorgio, the Army think it is quite safe. Do you know, they have never lost a single patient while they were being flown out? And they were badly wounded, I'm not!' Victoria smiled, attempting reassurance. 'I can help them, on the flight, and I'll send you word, as soon as I can. I promise.'

Their eyes met, and she knew that Chiara and Guiditta were right, his look was full of affection and more. But he only said, 'I'll miss you, cousin.'

The last days flew by in a flurry of cleaning and re-organizing at the villa, which was looking very dilapidated after the attentions of both the German and the United States armies. It seemed no time at all before Victoria and Guiditta were watching the last patients being carefully loaded into the waiting ambulances. The previous evening they had received an unexpected visit from Giorgio, Chiara and Julio, who had all come to say their goodbyes and wish her well for the journey. Chiara was beginning to show her pregnancy now, and Victoria drew her aside to promise her that as soon as she knew the post was working properly again, she would send off some baby clothes from the US.

'There are sure to be some nice things available at home,' she said. 'I'll get my mother onto it, she's good at that sort of thing. You won't be able to get much here for ages yet.'

Chiara had smiled her thanks, and seemed genuinely sad at their parting. She did not mention that several friends and relatives were already knitting for her, having unraveled old carefully stored baby clothes to provide the wool. 'When things are different,' she said, 'when it is safe, I promise I will bring the baby to see you.'

Julio had given her an embarrassed kiss, but Giorgio hugged her tightly, and then kissed her soundly on both cheeks. 'Remember, Victoria,' he said intently, 'you have two homes now, and two families. One in New York, and one here. Do not forget us.'

'I shall never forget you all, and Italy, and your kindness to me. I shall be back, don't worry. But I don't think I have two families, Giorgio. Because of Chiara's baby, I think we are all one.'

Victoria recalled the parting with genuine regret, as she acknowledged it was probably true – she felt as if she belonged here, as well as New York. But there was no time for reflection, the last two patients had been loaded into one special ambulance, and she was to go in that one with the senior nurse, as both patients needed constant attention. Guiditta, who had been holding back the tears since early morning, now gave up the attempt, allowing them to course down her face as she gave Victoria a last hug.

'Don't worry about anything here,' she said. 'I will make sure the villa is back to normal, bit at a time….'

'I know you will,' Victoria said, and it was true. They had spent the last few days making a full list of all that was to be done. 'You have the list if you are in doubt, and when the post gets back to normal you can let me know how it goes. Your pay will be at the bank every month, if anything goes wrong let me know … or better still …' she smiled, '… let Giorgio know and he will soon sort it out.'

They both laughed, and Guiditta whispered, 'He is a good man, Victoria, but I think you are remembering Guy, aren't you?'

It was a shock to hear his name, and Victoria could not reply. She gave a brief nod, and then she was climbing into the ambulance and they were handing up her suitcase. The ambulance pulled away and she watched and waved to Guiditta from the back window as they traveled down the drive until turning left onto the main road, and then she lost sight of the villa and her beloved friend behind the trees.

CHAPTER NINETEEN

Victoria was not able to see much from the small window of the ambulance but her patient, a fair haired young man named Ted Goddard, was sedated and mercifully asleep, and so she was able to glimpse a few last impressions of Rome as they traveled through. It was a bedraggled and unkempt city, far from the proud venue so extolled by tourists just a few years ago. It was as if the ancient buildings hung their heads in shame, their dirty windows and dilapidated shutters unable to meet the strong gaze of the sun, which sought out the ravages of recent times, and exposed them to the light at last.

'What a pity!' the senior nurse exclaimed. Victoria knew her as Sally, she had a good reputation at the villa for efficiency and hard work, but they had not worked together closely. Sally was from Detroit, in her forties perhaps, and true to her reputation seemed so capable and organized that Victoria immediately felt at ease. 'Never mind,' Sally continued, gazing out of the window, 'at least it's not bombed to buggery like some places.'

She adjusted the strapping on her patient's restraining belt, and smiled as he said quietly, 'Thanks, that's better.'

'OK, Dave. See if you can sleep now.' She turned to Victoria. 'I was here years ago, you know, for a visit. I must only have been about fifteen.'

Victoria was amazed. She couldn't imagine Sally ever having been fifteen. 'Really?'

'Yes, came with my family for a visit. My Dad is Italian extraction, although he was born in Detroit. We came by sea, of course, and it was such a hoot for me and my brothers. We thought Rome was just wonderful … and it was….'

Victoria wanted to ask about the brothers, *where were they now?* But it was better not to ask these days, and most likely Sally didn't know anyway, just as she couldn't imagine where Guy was. She tried to imagine him – *just at this minute, what is he doing? Is he alright, is he safe?*

Sally seemed to have heard her thoughts. 'My eldest brother is at home helping my dad. We have a bakery business.' He was too old to join up, but my younger brother; I don't know where he is now, not exactly. Somewhere in the Pacific….'

'Oh God,' Victoria thought. *This is an awful thing, this war, a bloody, bloody, bloody awful thing. I've hardly thought about the Pacific, and all those men fighting the Japanese, I've only concentrated on what is here, under my nose.*

'Have you heard any news lately?' she said. 'We heard very little at the villa, and of course, the Army staff weren't allowed to tell us anything much.'

'Only about the heavy fighting going on in France,' Sally replied. 'Since the landings in Normandy that is all there seems to be in the papers, hardly anything about the Pacific. The local paper was full of the massacre, of course, the Ardeatine caves, you heard about that?'

'Yes, briefly. Do they know more now?'

'As soon as we got to Rome we were besieged by people asking questions. Not at the villa, of course, I mean the Army generally. We were only interested in pushing on through Rome and driving the Germans out of Italy, but we did what we could to help. It was a reprisal, of course, ten hostages for every German soldier who died, and that meant over three hundred apparently. The ten for one instruction came directly from Hitler, so they say.'

'What an awful thing.' She could hardly bear to imagine it, the stark reality of it.

'Yes,' Sally said, and smiled down at Dave, who was asleep.

As the ambulance progressed through the city suburbs and then on into the countryside, it was plain that Rome had been made an exception. Small towns and villages had been demolished to the point where they were hardly recognizable as places of habitation at all. Everywhere, blackened ruins and charred landscapes stood ghastly testament to the hard fought battles which had taken place there. Most seemed deserted apart from a few straggling groups of desperate locals, trying to save something, anything, from the chaos. It went on for mile after mile, and Victoria eventually turned away, unable to face any more evidence of man's inhumanity. But then the only thing to look at was her patient, and young Ted Goddard was even worse evidence of the same thing, having lost both legs, one above and one just below the knee, and his right ear. The thick bandage around his head gave him a somewhat rakish air, which suited him, Victoria thought, as Ted was known to be a bit of a wag, and always ready for a laugh.

It was a few moments before she realized she was crying, and she mopped her eyes hastily in case Sally should see. But Sally had already noticed, and said quietly, 'Come on now, we're the lucky ones, we're going home.'

It was a long journey to the airfield at Foggia, and by the time they got there Victoria was tired. Both patients had needed Sally's expert attendance with the morphine and her own with the bedpan. She had expected the place to be more or less deserted, but it seemed frantically busy, with several planes being serviced and hundreds of men in uniform lying around waiting to be shipped home. They were the so-called "walking wounded," although some of them would have been hard pushed to walk very far.

About fifty of these men were loaded into the front of the C47 transport plane which was their ticket on the first leg of the journey home. Some were whooping and laughing with joy, others silent and grimacing with pain, showing a look of quiet desperation, as if they feared someone would change their minds and they would have to get off again. They hunkered down without complaint, some with seats and some on the floor. Before Major Simons did his last check, there was time for Sally and Victoria to take it in turns to eat at the airfield canteen before they finally took off for Tunis.

As the plane soared away from the runway Victoria felt a sense of relief and happiness – *I am going home!* However, there was also something else, a sense of sadness and loss in parting from this ravaged but much loved country, where her father had been born and lived, the father she had never known; and whether she liked it or not, where some of her own newly discovered family remained.

Years later, Victoria was to remember very little of that first leg of the journey back to the USA. In her memory, the hours dissolved into a hazy collection of recurring images which imprinted themselves forever onto her tired mind. Chief among these was the kind but exhausted face of Major Simons as he hovered, checking, forever checking, the quiet moans of Ted Goddard as he attempted to move and make himself more comfortable, and the occasional quiet monotones from the men at the front of the plane. They made no fuss; they were on their way home and still didn't quite believe it. At one point, Victoria woke suddenly, realizing she had been dozing in her seat. She blinked in confusion and Sally's voice insisted, 'Go back to sleep for a little, I'm here, I'll wake you later.' Then the warmth of a rough army blanket covered her, and she subsided into darkness once again.

When they eventually arrived, Tunis was much like the airfield at Foggia, efficient disembarkation, the patients transferred to the temporary US Army hospital, and she and Sally being fed in the staff canteen, before being shown their sleeping quarters; two bunks in the nurses' dormitory.

As they climbed into the bunks, Victoria murmured, 'What happens next?'

Sally snuggled down and closed her eyes. 'We just wait for someone to tell us where and when we report for the next flight.'

'And will that be to the USA?'

'Probably not. Depends on the plane. More likely we'll touch down in England … or Scotland….'

'What? I might be able to see my relatives there….'

'Don't get excited. You won't be allowed to leave the airfield. We're in transit and have to stay in

US territory ... probably just refueling and then on home....' Sally's voice faded, she was already asleep.

Prestwick, it was called, and they were only there a few hours, just enough time to re-fuel and for Victoria to be able to say she had actually been to Scotland. She didn't see anything which remotely suggested she was anywhere other than the now familiar US Army Air base. To her pleasure, she was reunited with Ted Goddard, apparently someone in the echelons of power had gotten it right for once and he and Dave were to travel the last leg home together, in the care of their original nursing team. There was a new doctor in charge however, and they were unable to find out what had happened to Major Simons. Sally explained that as well as the flights from Tunis, many of the wounded were sent home by sea, and so Major Simons may well be taking the long way home.

It was a long but uneventful flight which ended in the grey mist of an autumn dawn in the USA. Victoria hadn't known what to expect but it wasn't this ... hardly anyone around, just a steady stream of waiting ambulances staffed by kind but efficient doctors and nurses. As they piled into their staff cars and trucks the sun broke through with a golden light and Sally said, 'Looks like it's gonna be a hot day.' She settled herself in the back of a car and motioned Victoria to join her. 'Come on, let's get away for a meal and a shower, then we can have a real good sleep.'

Victoria climbed in, watching with concern as the patients were transferred. She could not imagine leaving them, what was happening to Ted?

Sally leaned forward and spoke to the driver, then turned to Victoria. 'It's OK,' she said. 'Relax, it's all over for us now. They are in really good hands, we've done our bit.' Seeing Victoria's face, she went on, 'Don't worry, the doctors go with them for the handover, Ted and Dave are OK, and all the others. I know how you feel, I couldn't bear to let them go the first time I did this run.'

'We didn't have time to say goodbye even….'

Sally laughed. 'They don't care about goodbyes, it's the hellos they're looking forward to.' She took off her uniform cap and pulled out a couple hairpins, and long blonde hair streamed onto her shoulders.

Victoria tried not to stare, and asked, 'Where are we exactly? And what do I do now?'

'We are at a US Army Air base somewhere in the United States of America. That's all we know officially. As Major Simons originally told us, we are still under strict security. That will still apply when you get home, too,' she added.

'Yes, I realize that. But how am I going to get home from here if I don't know where "here" is?'

Sally laughed. 'Oh, I expect you'll be debriefed, the same as everyone else. To put your mind at rest, it isn't going to take you too long to get home from here. We are at Mitchel Field, on the outskirts of New York.'

CHAPTER TWENTY

Two days later, Victoria's train pulled into Grand Central Station in New York. She had managed to have a short telephone conversation with her mother to give her arrival time, but they had been cut off and she had no idea if she would be met.

As she stepped down from the train with her battered suitcase, she looked this way and that. The place was swarming with people, but she was momentarily overwhelmed by the beautiful familiarity of the lovely building. Surely they would come if they could…?

Suddenly, he was there … her darling Dada … dashing towards her and beaming like a Cheshire cat. He was the same, perhaps slightly older and a little greyer, but still outstandingly handsome, his arms opening wide and his face a picture of sheer joy.

'Will ye look at the darlin' little one!' The Irish accent, now overlaid with nuances of New York, was always more pronounced when he was excited. She flung herself at him.

'Oh, Dada … my dada….' she whispered, as she felt herself enveloped in the big arms. Once more she was as she had always been, his "darlin' little one", the name which had stuck ever since the day when, as a tiny child, her great uncle Vittorio had handed her to Clancy Sullivan for safe-keeping.

And safe-keeping she had received, she thought, watching as he commandeered her suitcase and organized her through a side entrance to where the big Buick stood waiting. How lovely to have him in charge. Dada, who knew everything about everything under the sun, or at least that is how she had always thought of him, always understood him, as the rock upon which life itself depended. Now the rock settled himself into the back seat alongside her as the smiling chauffeur closed the door, and Clancy Sullivan turned to her again with that big smile.

'Let me take a proper look,' he commanded. He took her face in his hands and looked her over carefully, and she saw the love in his eyes, and also perhaps…? Perhaps a little sadness?

'It's wonderful to have you home again, darlin'. We could hardly believe it when we got the phone call. You're looking well, but a bit thinner.' He held on to her face, examining her minutely. 'I'm not sure you're my little girl any more, I think ye're all grown up, darlin'.'

'Oh, Dada, I think I have grown up, quite a lot in fact. But I'll always be your little girl, if I live to be ninety!'

'Of course you will, and before you ask, your Mom isn't here because she is practically re-designing the house to prepare for you!' He tapped on the chauffeur's window. 'OK John, we'd better be off, I'm under strict instructions to take you straight home mind.'

They both laughed, remembering the same things, how her Dada had often gotten into trouble with Mom when after picking her up from school, he would take her for ice cream, or to see the ducks in the park, instead of straight home. But how she treasured those stolen half hours, she recalled, when she would tell all her small girlish troubles to Dada as they fed the ducks, and he would take it all very seriously and they would talk about it, until he told a joke and they would both start laughing and be as silly as they wanted.

'Oh, Dada,' she said, catching his hand to her, 'it is so good to be home, you've no idea.'

The beautiful old brownstone house looked just as she remembered it, and Victoria scrambled up the steps just as the door opened and her Mom came out. They stood and looked at each other, and then the tears came before they even embraced, tears of joy and tears of sadness, for they both knew that they would have to face it before too long, they would have to talk about James. But for now they both hastily dried their tears, knowing this was not the time, not yet. First, there must be the preliminaries, talk about the journey, and the luck that she had been given the Army flights home, and how Dada's health had been not so good lately, and didn't she want to see her room, waiting for her like always?

Through all this, Mom chattered away as if it mattered, and Victoria had to admit that her mother, who had always been an acknowledged beauty, was at last showing a few signs of aging; a crease or two at the corners of her eyes, a little tautness at the neck, but most noticeable was a gentle hesitation, a lack of certainty in her manner, which had never been there before. *Perhaps it takes the loss of a child,* she thought, *to do that to Mother, she who was always so positive, so determined. The loss of a child, a real child, a blood relative, as Giorgio would say.*

Over dinner and her joy at eating her mother's cooking again, the conversation continued and Victoria found plenty to tell them about the villa, and Guiditta, and her first two years in Italy, and how she had found she couldn't get home once the Germans arrived.

'I became Luisa Vetti,' she told them. 'It was so lucky you had thought when I was young to give me dual nationality. I was able to fit in quite easily with Giorgio's help, especially as I spoke good Italian.'

'The Swiss finishing school fees weren't wasted then?' Dada said, rather sarcastically.

'Oh, Dada! The school was wonderful, but it couldn't prepare me for what happened later, I don't think anything could have....'

And so it began, the story of how Guy came to see them and how Victoria learned about James. About their meeting in the cave and the fun they had, she knew it was important, to tell them about the fun....

It was quite late before she had said it all, she had decided on the train to tell them the whole truth, and to leave nothing out. She had not wanted to tell it all, not about Fleischer and the attempted rape, not about James staying behind in the thick of the firing, but she had a strong feeling that it was their *right* to know, that any attempt to sugar the pill would be misguided. So it came out, haltingly, bit by horrendous bit, until she was scrambling away across the field with Guiditta and Chiara and Julio, and Guy with the heavy pack, and James was holding off the pursuing Germans, and then ... and then....

Looking at their horrified faces, she knew she couldn't stop there, but she couldn't go on either, because she didn't know with any certainty what had happened at the villa afterwards.

'We only got news from Giorgio,' she said, and explained then about sheltering in the mountains with Alfonso and Maria, and what Giorgio had come to tell them when the Germans eventually left the villa, and Rome.

'I asked about his body,' Mom said. 'But the Army could tell me nothing. They just said it was "unlikely" he would ever be found. How can that be?'

'Unfortunately it is all too common,' Victoria said. 'There was another man killed that night, he was called Paolo, the kitchen man who helped James and Guy get away. He put the big trash can under the window so they could climb down, and he was caught. His body has not been found either, or indeed that of Fleischer.'

Dada was quiet and thoughtful. 'Is there any chance, any likelihood, that James survived? That perhaps they took him with them when they left, as a prisoner?'

'No Dada, I am sure not. I spoke to Giorgio about the possibility, and he was sure there was not. When they left they were panicking, they were not in the mood to take prisoners.'

Dada nodded gently.

'I want you both to know that I understand that I made a huge mistake that night, and that a lot of the blame is mine....' *There, I've said it, I managed to get it out. They must know ... they have a right to know....'*

'If I had kept Fleischer occupied we might have all gotten away, it is a possibility at least.'

Her mother looked shocked, and Dada had a look of horror on his face.

'But it was Guiditta who shot Fleischer, and woke everyone up,' her mother said. 'You never had the chance.'

'Guiditta only shot him because I was fighting him,' Victoria explained. 'I could have signaled her not to do it, but I didn't….'

'And she was right,' said her mother vehemently. 'Give Guiditta a medal, I say!'

'Your mother is right,' said Clancy. 'In the heat of the moment like that, there is no time for working out the pros and cons. Guiditta did what she had to do, so she did, there is no point in your getting upset and feeling guilty about it, these things happen in wartime.'

They went over and over it all and came to the same conclusion, and by then Victoria was so tired she could hardly think. Her wonderful parents consoled her and talked to her, but when she lay in bed, she couldn't help but reflect that it was James, the beloved *blood relative, their real child,* who had died, and she had survived, who was no relative at all.

CHAPTER TWENTY-ONE

Although she spent the best part of that first week asleep, it slowly dawned on Victoria that home was not the place it used to be. Like everything else in the world, it had changed because of this damned war. Her mother for instance, who seemed to be working about eighty hours a week, in spite of being worried about the safety of her immediate family in England; which, according to the daily newscasts, had been "bombed to buggery," to use Sally's apt phrase. This was quite a turn-around.

Anna Sullivan, the elegant wife of the rich restaurant and hotel owner, Clancy Sullivan, who had been referred to as "that woman" by New York Society for years, was now very much in demand because of her work for War Charities and fund raising activities. Indeed, if you wanted ten thousand food parcels organized, or the money raised to pay for them, Anna Sullivan was guaranteed to be the best contact. She was a born administrator, and if she undertook to do something, it happened.

The phrase "that woman" became gently obscured, to be replaced by phrases like "That wonderful Anna Sullivan," and "Sullivan's wife, the War Fundraiser." She was reputed to have raised huge sums for War Bonds, and some of the wilder rumors even darkly suggested that she "had persuaded her Mafia friends to stump up millions." Most of it was untrue, of course, even the earlier description of her as "that woman" was based on rumor which was largely false; her husband's slight involvement with Vittorio Vetti had been for the purpose of saving his son's life, and no other.

But New York society loved its scandal-mongering and it had continued for years, until at length the wealth and organizing ability of Clancy and Anna Sullivan had made itself available to an approved purpose. Some of the higher echelons of New York society, however, still predictably continued their disdain for the Sullivans. It was pointed out that they were, in fact, *"nobodies,"* English immigrants (and not notable ones either!) who had arrived without a bean and made their pile in trade. This was enough to put off certain people for life, but it was also said that Clancy Sullivan had worked on a building site and that his wife had scrubbed floors in the early days. These people would never under any circumstances have admitted the Sullivans to their distant acquaintance, never mind their homes. The free and open society of the greatest city in the world was not without its own strata of snobbery, but the slightly less exalted supporters of *"our guys out there"* who had money to give, gave it happily to Anna Sullivan as the needs of the present war effort became ever more demanding.

Victoria did not quite understand what had happened in the four years she had been away, but one evening as she sat with Dada after dinner, waiting for Mom to come home from another everlasting campaign meeting, he explained his thoughts to her, in his own inimical way, with much laughter and sardonic comment.

'It is funny, so it is,' Clancy said. 'A few years ago my money was "dirty money" and I couldn't give it away ... well, to a few charities perhaps, ones that really needed it. Now, your mother smiles and we are asked to dine at some of the best houses! Often I don't want to go, I have been snubbed in the past and now suddenly they act like I am their best friend! Your Mom and I have had a few arguments over it, so we have. But you know what she's like....'

'She can wind you round her little finger, is that what you mean, Dada?'

'Certainly not! Well perhaps...! Anyway we go, and I behave as best I can. It's for a good cause, that's what I keep telling meself, otherwise I'd tell them to go hang, so I would.'

'Oh, Dada! I can't imagine you trying to behave yourself ... I would like to see that! But I don't suppose I'll ever be invited to any of these affairs.'

'Of course you will! Now people are getting to know you are home at last, they will want to see you, darlin'.'

'And hear about my inheritance from my Mafioso uncle? I don't think so! I can hardly tell them I was looked after by a present Mafia boss when I was in Italy, and was nearly raped by a German officer....'

'Oh, my God! I see what ye mean!' Clancy's eyes sparkled and he began that infectious giggle she loved so much. 'How about that, though? What a party piece, do you think we could do it? We could cause an uproar, so we could!' He began to laugh out loud and Victoria joined in, and they laughed and giggled until Clancy suddenly stopped, wiping his eyes. He shook his head and Victoria saw he was close to tears.

'Doesn't seem right, does it? Laughing like that, so soon after James?'

'Oh, Dada, James would be the first one to want us to laugh ... he was always full of fun.'

'True enough. Always good for a laugh, so he was. And you know, darlin', there was a time I blamed him for that. When he was younger, he was a bit on the wild side, and I used to try to make him knuckle down, you know? God, if I only had him back ... only had him here, he could be as wild as he liked....'

'I know, Dada, I know,' she soothed, noticing the lines around his eyes. Yes, it had hit him hard. She said, 'He still was a bit wild, I think. In Italy, I mean. I know his friend Guy thought he was, anyway. And Giorgio certainly thought he was. It was part of James, taking risks, doing the unexpected....'

'Why did this Mafia bloke, Giorgio, think that?'

'I know he thought our raid on the villa was a bit too risky. He didn't want me or Guiditta involved at all in the beginning.'

'He may have been right about that.'

'Yes, possibly. But we did get the documents they wanted, and that was James's orders. Guy got them to HQ.'

'And were they useful? Was it all worth it?' Clancy was intense.

'I have no idea. The Germans left Rome anyway shortly afterwards as the Allies advanced.' Victoria became distraught, remembering. 'Oh, Dada, you should have seen those poor men at the villa, so many awful injuries, and they were the lucky ones, they had survived.... It was awful, Dada, and those poor people who were shot in the Ardeatine ... over three hundred....'

'Yes, darlin', you told us.' Clancy leaned forward in his chair. 'You have been through such a lot....'

'No! It was nothing to what some people are going through there. Even now the Germans are gone there's nothing to eat, and I have come away and left them to it!' Victoria began to cry. 'Please try to understand, Dada. They were so kind to me, Guiditta and Giorgio and Chiara and Julio and the others, and whether we like it or not they are my family, my blood relations....'

'Ah!' Clancy said gently. 'Is that a phrase of Giorgio's? *Blood relations?*'

'Yes, I suppose so, I hadn't thought much about it before, but it's true, isn't it?'

'Yes, it's true. And it is a phrase your great uncle Vittorio liked to use. They set great store by it, you know.'

'Who do?'

'Italian people. They set great store by family.'

'Do you mean Mafia people?'

Clancy looked surprised. 'I don't know. Perhaps. But I've never known many.' He smiled. 'An old Irish immigrant like me, with no relatives to speak of, wouldn't know much about such things ... mind you, I have two cousins who went to California, but we lost touch....'

He smiled again. 'The main thing is, darlin', that they were kind to you, so they were. That is the important thing. They cared for you and looked after you, but have you asked yourself the obvious question?'

'And what is that?' Victoria asked, intrigued.

'Would they have looked after you the way they did if you had not been *blood relations?*'

Victoria came down late to breakfast after a troubled night. She had lain awake wondering about

Guy. Was he still in France? And if so, where? The news media spoke of advances and setbacks with such regularity it was hard to know whether progress was being made or not. The Russians were certainly doing their part by advancing well on the eastern front, and overall the news seemed good, although the casualty lists made dark reading.

To her surprise her parents were both still at the breakfast table, which was unusual. Her mother rose, she was still in her dressing gown. 'Good morning, love, I'll put you an egg on, the coffee's still good,'

'Thanks.' Victoria slid into her seat. 'I'm surprised to see you both here. No work today, Dada?'

'The boss can take a day off when he wants to, so he can. Especially when he has his daughter home.'

'And I've nothing until a meeting at three,' her mother said. 'To tell the truth, love….' She looked at Clancy, and Victoria saw agreement pass between them. They had a sort of telepathy, she thought, wondering how they did it.

'We want … we want … to have a little talk to you….'

'Oh no!' Shades of old exam results and unruly behavior raised their ugly heads. 'Aren't I a bit old for that now?' She was joking, but her mother did not respond.

'It's nothing like that. Just something we feel we ought to tell you.'

'Why? What's happened?'

'Nothing! Nothing's happened, darlin'. Her father took over. 'It's just something we have decided to tell you, we feel you are old enough, and mature enough, to understand.'

'What?' *Not another bloody family secret, for goodness sake!* 'Is it something about uncle Vittorio, something to do with what we talked about last night?'

'No, not directly, but our talk made me think we should be honest with you. It's clear that meeting your birth family has made a big impact on you, of course it has, and we want to help if we can.'

For once her father seemed serious, and Victoria decided to shut up, but mentally her hackles were up and she knew that if they dared ... *if they dared* to criticize anyone in Italy she would surely explode, she wouldn't be able to help it.

'So, this thing you're going to tell me, did James know about it?'

That look between them again, and a little wince of pain from Mom. 'No,' she said quietly, 'but it is about James.'

The blood drained from Victoria's face. 'They haven't found....'

'No! No dear, nothing like that. This is about years ago, when your dad and I first knew each other in England.'

Another glance at Clancy, who nodded.

'Before we were married,' her mother continued, 'I had an affair.' She waited for the moment of shock to subside and then went on, slowly and with purpose, so that she would get it right, and make her daughter understand. 'It was one of those silly things; I thought I was in love....'

'Was this when you were in France?' Victoria knew her mother had spent some time in France working for an artists' colony in Brittany. It was not a secret, but she had never talked about it much. Suddenly Victoria knew why. The first thing that entered her mind was the painting, the big canvas that hung in the lounge, the one of her mother sitting on a terrace peeling vegetables, painted when she was in France. It was a family treasure.

'Did he paint the picture in the lounge? This man you had the affair with? Did he do that picture?'

'No, he didn't.' Her mother looked at her in surprise, as if to say, *what would you do about it if he did?*

'No,' her mother continued gently. 'He did not paint that picture; it was done by one of the other artists there, a young woman from the Balkans. She gave it to me as a leaving gift.' She sighed, and then continued: 'But you are right, the affair was in France, and with one of the artists there. It doesn't matter who he was really, he died many years ago. The main thing is ... what we wanted you to know ... is that I became pregnant there.'

'Go on.' Victoria glanced at her father and he smiled at her, trying to reassure as always. *How can he bear this?*

'When I told him about the baby, he didn't want to know. It transpired he was already engaged to someone ... someone more of his class. I came home in disgrace, to the wrath of my father. My brother Will was the one who cared for me and told Clancy what had happened.'

The room was quiet and Victoria said, 'I always knew I loved old Uncle Will for some good reason.'

'Ay,' Clancy broke in. 'He's always been a good chap, so he has....'

'And this good chap married me,' said her mother softly. 'He asked me to marry him and go with him to America right away. In that way no one, except us and Will of course, would know that the baby wasn't his.'

The penny finally dropped. 'You mean that James ... James –'

'Yes, James was not what you call my *blood relation,*' said Clancy. 'Your mother was his birth mother, but I was not his father. We decided never to tell James about this, he had been mine since he was born and my name is on his birth certificate. We wanted him always to feel secure and loved, and believe me; I loved him as only a father could.'

Anna Sullivan reached across to take her husband's hand as the tears coursed down his face. Victoria was both amazed and moved, and found it hard to understand how this knowledge altered her own feelings about James. She had always regarded him as her brother, but knew of course, that he was not her *blood* brother. Now it seemed he was not even that, but was a half-brother by adoption, whatever that meant. Did it matter? Of course not, James was James, and always would be her lovely fun-loving brother, always in some trouble of some sort, and at the end turning out to be a hero….

They were all crying by this time, and after some hugs and attempts to console each other, her mother suddenly said, 'Gosh, Victoria, I forgot your egg! It's boiled dry. I'll do another one….'

Victoria smiled. 'I'll have it as it is, Mom. I like hard boiled eggs, I would have been thrilled to have this in Italy.'

CHAPTER TWENTY-TWO

Victoria pondered at length on what her parents had disclosed about James's birth. Her father had disappeared off to his office, but she caught her Mom as she emerged from her dressing room after lunch, looking every inch the elegant businesswoman.

'Mom, do you think we could talk a little more?' she asked.

Her mother smiled and said, 'Of course, I don't have to leave for at least an hour, let's go into the lounge.'

Victoria wanted to know about Anna's time in France, and they looked again at the painting which showed her as she was then, so young and pretty, but with a hint of the deep beauty which was to develop later.

'Why did you decide to tell me now?' Victoria said at last. She wanted to ask, *why tell me at all?* but sensed there must be a reason.

'Well, after your talk with Dada last night, he told me he felt you were a little upset. No, not upset … confused, I think that's what he said. You had been talking about what you called your "blood relations" in Italy, and your Dada wanted you to understand that it is what people do that matters, more than who they are. You have always known that it never made any difference to us whether or not you were a *blood relation,* but sometimes it isn't easy to understand something which is so personal to yourself. You know about this family, how it works, how we always act towards each other, and we thought if we told you about James's birth, it might help you to see things more clearly. Has it, do you think?'

'I'm not sure,' Victoria said. 'But Dada is right, I have been feeling confused. Before I went to Italy I was always quite sure who I was, where I came from. I knew that my birth parents had died, of course, and they were like a story I had become used to, familiar but not really affecting me in any real way. My life, who I was and where I lived, and how I felt, was always quite clear. You were my parents and James was my brother, and ... oh, Mom! He was a good brother to me! I have been thinking so much about him, little things that happened when we were young, and he was always kind to me, always.' She hesitated, and then said, 'In Italy, I came to realize that there are other people, living people, involved in the story, the old story I have known since I was a child. It affected them too, and they haven't forgotten it, they haven't forgotten me! I seem to have some sort of place there as well, and there seem to be expectations of me, so that I'm not quite sure who I am any more. One thing hasn't changed though, I can't ever think of James as anything other than my brother, and I always will.'

'Good,' Anna said. 'And to James, you were always his darling little sister. It never occurred to him that your birth made any difference to that simple fact. And I hope you will always feel the same about Dada and me, we are your parents and always will be, no matter what. That doesn't mean there can't be room in your life to love other people too, people like Chiara and her baby ... James's baby....' Anna was tearful now.

'But not Giorgio. Dada hates him, doesn't he? Like he hated uncle Vittorio?'

Her mom smiled. 'I don't think your Dada could hate anyone if he tried! No, he doesn't hate Giorgio, he's never met him. I think it is just that he fears for you, don't forget we have experience of what getting involved with these people can mean.'

'You mean the Mafia? In Italy they don't call themselves that, they –'

'It doesn't matter what they are called, Victoria! As your Dada says, it is what they do that matters.'

'And what they did was take care of me, Mom,' Victoria said quietly. 'I think I may have starved if Giorgio hadn't done what he could.'

'And don't think I'm not grateful for that,' Anna said. 'I doubt I'll ever get over James's death, but thank God I have you, my darling daughter. You have always made me so proud of you.'

'Well, as to that,' Victoria said, 'I know I'm going to regret this, but could you do with an extra volunteer? Something to do with war work? I can't sit here twiddling my thumbs while everyone else is doing their bit.'

'Fund raising? Or practical stuff? That means packing food parcels,' Anna explained.

'Food parcels, please.'

'Good. You start tomorrow.'

A few minutes after Anna left for her meeting, the front door bell rang. It was the postman, who was not enjoying his day. 'Is there a Victoria Sullivan Vetti here?' he asked. 'I can hardly make head or tail of this address.'

'Yes, that's me,' said Victoria happily. It could only be from Guy....

It was not from Guy. As soon as she saw the hand and the postmark, she knew it was from Italy. The post must be working again.

Inside there was a note from Chiara, and another smaller envelope, addressed in Guy's hand, to the villa. Chiara wrote:

This came for you a few days after you left, I think it is from Guy. I hope you had a good journey home and are safe there now. We are all well here, and things are slowly improving at the villa. Giorgio is trying to get some paint, but it isn't easy. I am at the villa helping Guiditta, things did not work out at the school, once they found out about the baby they did not want me to work there after all. I am a bad example to the children apparently. Our dearest love to you,

Chiara.

Poor Chiara, Victoria thought. *How must she feel about that? Perhaps Guiditta was right, it will be difficult for her.* She sat down in the lounge to read the enclosed letter. It was only two pages, and some of the words had been deleted by the censor, as had the address at the top.

My dear Victoria and Guiditta,

I expect by the time you read this you will have become used to the US Army being around at the villa, (of course, he doesn't know, she thought) *rather like the people who live here in XXXXXXXXX have become used to having the US Army billeted on them. I must say I like the Dutch* (so he was not in France at all!) *they have made us so very welcome. We are able to help them with some decent food and they show us some home comfort and normality, which is very welcome I can assure you. When we left*

our last place a few old ladies there cried and kissed us, the children too, they are all so glad to be rid of the Boche. Our days are either very boring or a real nightmare, today is boring, all equipment has to be combat ready so that means cleaning and checking your kit ten times over. The push towards the XXXXXXXXX XXXX continues, (Siegfried Line, she thought, having scoured the New York Times) *we are hoping to be in XXXXXXX before too long, although I can't say I'm looking forward to it. Don't reply to this letter as no doubt we shall have moved on, can't give you an address at the moment. I often think of you both and the lovely countryside around the villa, and Alfonso and Maria's farm. I don't expect to ever be back there but shall not forget it, and the kindness of our friends there, and especially you, Victoria.*
See you in New York,
Love Guy.

Especially you, Victoria! She hugged the paper to her and enjoyed a few seconds of elation before the questions began. Of course, by now he could be in Germany already ... or not ... or France ... or wounded...or.... Stop, she told herself, this way lies madness. No kisses ... but he did write "especially you, Victoria."

What did that mean? Especially you, Victoria. Did it mean anything at all, or was it just something to say, something to write to someone you like but don't really know very well? Because that was the truth, they didn't know each other very well. It had been over six months since she had seen him, since that awful day when he had left Alfonso's farm, almost bent double by that great heavy back pack, and each day she had thought of him, wondered about him, where he was, what he was doing, praying he was safe.

She began to wonder if she would ever see him again. Although they had said "See you in New York", did that really mean anything? She scoured the casualty lists but that didn't mean anything either. She thought back to a particular evening at the cave, when they had stood together briefly – *when had it ever been other than briefly?* They had looked at the stars, and he had pointed out some of them and the names, none of which she could now remember. She had thought it romantic at the time, had *felt* it was romantic, but had he felt the same? Would she ever see that look again, as he turned his head, that look of frank interest, teasing and smiling at the same time?

Probably not, she had to concede. What had happened had changed them, both of them. She knew she was not the same person who had so happily visited her inherited villa with such big ideas. And Guy had been through so much more, even now he could be in the thick of battle and how would she know? If he came home, he would be changed forever. But what was to be done, that was the point. What could be done?

Only wait, and pack food parcels, she thought. Christmas was coming ever nearer, and how it would be possible to get through it, she couldn't imagine. Images of her Dada and James coming home with a huge Christmas tree intruded on her thoughts. They had been such happy times, lots of laughter, and Mom complaining about the mess, and Dada sweeping her off her feet to dance around the tree. Would they have a tree this year? Not much point, it would be different if there were children.... Chiara's baby was due in late February or early March. She must try to send a few choice treats to them for Christmas, but she wasn't sure if they had received the last parcel.

She sat down and thought of Chiara and her baby, and the unkindness of the self- righteous who would not allow her back into the school. She knew Chiara would be alright, she had Giorgio, and Julio and Guiditta, and with the thought of these friends the tears came again, until she decided she must do something. She was not starting her voluntary work until tomorrow, so she would write to Guy via the Army post. You never know, it might just get to him, she reasoned. She didn't know where he was but he had given her his Army number. She would try the Red Cross as well, just in case.

CHAPTER TWENTY THREE

As Christmas approached, all eyes and ears seemed glued to news from the front in France, where at last the Allies were lined up, poised on the German border. On the 16th December, Hitler had launched a surprise dawn Blitzkrieg upon them from the cover of surrounding forest, trying to take the town of Bastogne in a maneuver designed to split the line. The Americans, under Brigadier General McAuliffe, fought back strongly for days, but by 20th December the Germans had what was described as a "ring of steel" around Bastogne.

In the United States, millions of people were hunched over small hastily drawn maps of the region from the local or national newspaper, trying to understand and identify day by day with this small town and its surroundings, where so many of their young men were holding the line against impossible odds. The Sullivan family was also following it keenly, as the town held out day after day, until on Christmas Eve, when Bastogne was heavily bombed by German planes, all seemed lost and there were many casualties, civilian and military. Somehow, the troops still held just a couple days longer, and when the news came that on Boxing Day General Patton's 3rd Army had managed to breach the ring and lift the siege, the relief and joy felt in millions of homes in Europe and the USA, and in the Sullivan household, was like the best Christmas present ever known.

Despite her misgivings, and the news from the front, Victoria found that Christmas came and went before she knew it. With the hard work at the packing factory and the extra duties that her mother seemed to find daily, life was busy if not fulfilling. They didn't have a tree, because apart from the fact they were rarely at home together to enjoy it, trees were hard to obtain like so much else. Christmas morning was a quiet and tearful event for the family, with all of them thinking of James, but in the afternoon they were run off their feet helping at a children's party Anna had organized for the local church. Clancy had been practically forced into playing Santa Claus by Anna, who exclaimed, 'You have to do it. There aren't enough men left for me to have a choice in the matter.'

The whole thing went off well, with messages from the front being read out by some of the families, many of which were the new V mail cards which were so much easier to send in both directions. 'You can't say much but at least you keep in touch,' was Anna's comment, 'and that is the main thing.'

Victoria wondered if a V mail would reach Guy…. As for "Peace on Earth", she thought, that was just a distant dream.

Victoria knew New York from childhood; knew its moods and business, knew its bustle and grey silences punctuated by traffic noise and sirens, and the everlasting underground rumble of city life. She had settled back easily into life here, like a homing pigeon, which of course, she was. Nevertheless, things were not the same, and in spite of the welcome news that General Patton had launched the offensive as soon as 29th December, the weighty dead hand of war hovered over everything. As the news from the front seeped through, and the casualty lists grew and supplies were more difficult to obtain, it seemed as if the huge city shrank gently into itself and the whole world was reduced to quietly working, working, working and waiting....

Sometimes Victoria wondered what she was waiting for. For Guy? How could she say she was waiting for him when she hardly knew him? And if he did come home safely, what then? Was he waiting for her?

It occurred to her that the only times she had spent with Guy were times of stress. Nothing had been ordinary, everyday. The time he first arrived at the cottage, the stolen few hours in the cave, a short time in the attic, and then the awful scramble through the mountains and that last day at Alfonso's farm. All of it (and there wasn't much), had been played out against the tension and constant fear of discovery. What she hoped she was waiting for was normality, getting to know you times, a walk in Central Park, a quiet dinner, a baseball game.

All true, all true, she thought, and then smiled to herself. It was true, but it was not all, not by any means. Yes, she was waiting for those quiet times, those getting to know each other times, but she wanted more than that. Much, much more. She wanted Guy, all of that happy and teasing nature and the smiling seriousness, she wanted to look into his eyes and never look away. She wanted to hold him in her arms and never let him go ... never ever .... She wanted to spend the rest of her life with him.

Why did she feel like this about a man she hardly knew? Was it because there wasn't anyone else around? She knew in her heart it was not. In that secret place within, where she had held and nurtured Guy's image for so long, she knew it was more than that.

In snowy February, daily life for Victoria became a mixture of sheer hard work, boredom and exhaustion. The only relief from the constant draining sameness was the family's attendance at a fund raising dinner, where they were seated at a circular table with a local attorney and political deal maker named Hiram J. Turner; notorious windbag and a longtime adversary of Clancy's. His wife, Barbara, was a vacuous little woman who had no conversation other than the dreadful scarcity of everything under the sun, including her favorite shade of lipstick and her preferred silk underwear.

'They say it's all to do with the war out East,' she said, waving with her diamond-studded fingers to show she knew roughly where East was situated. 'Not able to get the silk now, apparently. But I think it's all to do with putting up the prices for those of us who can afford to buy the best. After all, I suppose you can get silk anywhere if you look for it....'

Hiram J Turner's conversation (if it could be called a conversation as it only went one way) was much more of the moment. He spoke of the big wheeler-dealing situations in which he was sure to be closely concerned, managing to increase the volume when a notable Senator's name was mentioned so that he could be heard over several tables. Then he went on to the possible merging of three large companies, and the consequential benefit to their financial positioning which would occur "when this current war is over."

'Sounds like you think there'll be another one....' Clancy managed to squeeze in the comment.

'Bound to be, bound to be.' bellowed the sonorous Hiram. 'Good for business you see. You just gotta be sure you're in there, in the right kind of business at the right time.'

Victoria thought Clancy would explode, but just in time Anna rose to her feet in order to make the fund raising speech, which, having been long perfected by years of practice was humorous, to the point, and at its close, quite moving. To applause at the end, Clancy rose to support the speech, commenting on the quality of the meal and the conversation. 'I've been sitting here listening to one of our foremost attorneys,' he said with a smile at Hiram. 'And all I can say is, if he uses his check book as much as he uses his mouth, we're in for big money tonight, so we are!'

Victoria and Anna giggled all the way home.

They hardly had time to calculate the amount made from the dinner before Victoria arrived home late from a hard day packing food parcels. Anna was waiting for her, immaculate and elegant and dressed for the evening.

She handed Victoria an envelope. 'It's from Rome. Chiara's handwriting, I think.'

'Oh!' Victoria grabbed at it. 'Thanks. You could have opened it, Mom, I wouldn't have minded....' She hesitated. 'Are you going out?'

'No, we have a guest for dinner. A soldier, a G.I. on his way home from the front. He has to catch a train at 9.30 so I said we could eat early, and your Dada will take him to the train.'

'Who is he? How did this happen?'

'I've no idea. That is, I know his name; he's Clay Summersbee and he's from Wisconsin....'

'Oh I see, this is one of those "befriend a G.I things."'

'No, it isn't.' Anna sounded impatient. 'Victoria, do listen, please. He phoned this afternoon to say he had met Guy Waldman in Belgium, and Guy asked him to call on us and let us know he was OK.'

Oh, the pain! And then the sweet searing joy at the sound of his name.... Guy was OK! A warm glow surged through her body and she could hardly breathe.

'But what did he say? How did they meet? Is Guy coming home too?'

'Victoria, please. I don't know, we had hardly any conversation at all,' Anna explained patiently. 'Guy gave him our address and he looked us up in the phonebook. That's all I know. He said he knew very little, I don't think he knew Guy at all really. He didn't want to come to dinner, he just wanted to phone and give us the message and then get home. But I insisted, and when I said we could take him to the train he said he would come. It sounded like he's a bit lost and doesn't know his way around.'

'Let's hope he gets here then.'

'Yes, he's coming at seven and Dada is on his way from the office now, so will you please go and get ready, Victoria?' Anna took charge in her usual organized way. 'He's a G.I on his way home, and the least we can do is give him a welcome and a good meal. You can read your letter later....'

Victoria changed quickly and carefully, and brushed out her hair from the French plait style she wore for work. She quickly opened Chiara's letter, but had only a few moments to peruse it before she heard Dada arrive downstairs. Her mind in turmoil, she raced down to acquaint them with Chiara's news, but before she could speak the front door bell rang and Clancy opened it. The young G.I. who stood in the doorway was therefore met by three anxious faces, and couldn't fail to be aware of the stir he was causing.

'Come in, come in and welcome ... er ... Clay, isn't it?' Dada was doing his stuff although he had only just arrived himself.

The young man, a thin, gangly sort of youth who didn't look old enough to be in the Army, never mind a veteran, came in and shook hands with them. His uniform looked new and was clean and pressed, but he was obviously a little overwhelmed by his surroundings. When they had assembled in the lounge he immediately stammered, 'I ... I don't want you to get the wrong idea, I didn't know your son really....'

'That's alright, Clay, and just so you know, Guy Waldman isn't our son.' Dada almost faltered, but went on, 'He was a close friend of our son, who died last year in Italy. Victoria, our daughter, was there too and knows Guy, so of course we are very concerned about him.'

'Oh, I see,' Clay said, but it was obvious from his expression he didn't.

'Come and sit down, and make yourself comfortable,' Anna said, with a sharp glance at Victoria who was about to begin a barrage of questions. 'We'll have a drink before our dinner, and you can tell us what you do know.' She shot a look at Clancy, who immediately went to the drinks trolley. 'Whisky?' he asked Clay.

'Gosh yes, that would be great.'

As the drinks were given out, Clay began to relax. His glance continually strayed to Victoria, and it was obvious he was impressed. By the time they went in to dinner, he had explained he was with General Patton's Army and had been injured at the time of the relief of Bastogne. 'Not that you can see it,' he explained with a smile, pointing at his chest. 'The damage is all under the shirt. That's why I'm invalided out.'

Victoria was trying hard to keep from blurting out her questions – when had he met Guy?

As if in answer to her unspoken thoughts, Clay said, 'A bunch of us were on our way out of the field hospital, we were being sent to the main hospital for treatment and then we had been told we would be shipped home. Some of the other guys there were joshing us, you know, about going home ... and I shouted, 'New York here I come ... and then Wisconsin....'

Clay looked straight at Victoria. He swallowed. 'Then another lot of wounded came in, they were just coming in to the field hospital as we were leaving, they had been wounded in the siege and of course hadn't had any real medical help until they were relieved.' He swallowed again, the memory upset him. 'They were in a pretty bad state, I can tell you. Anyway, as I said I was showing off ... sort of ... shouting about New York, and this guy comes at me and says, real urgent like, 'You going to New York?' And I said yes I was, because I had to get the train there to get home, I knew that ... and he said, 'When you get there buddy, do me a favor... 'and he pulled this out of his pocket.' Clay reached into his breast pocket and displayed a crumpled photo. 'He said, 'get in touch with these folks and tell them I'm OK, the address is on the back'.'

Victoria stared at the small dirty scrap. She reached out and took it with a pang of recognition. It was the photograph of her and James outside the house, the one Guy had shown her when he first arrived at the cottage, the one he said he had taken from James's locker. 'Yes,' she whispered. 'I know Guy had this with him....'

'Well anyway,' Clay said, 'his leg was a real mess, and the sergeant was trying to get him on a trolley, and he wouldn't go because he was talking to me ... and he kept saying, 'My name is Guy Waldman, my name is Guy Waldman...' and the sergeant was shoving him and he started shoving back and I shouted, 'What shall I tell them?' and he shouted, 'Just tell them I'm fine, I'm fine....' And then I remember he said to the sergeant, 'Stop shoving me ... you're not the Boche.' It was so funny, really....'

'Funny?' It was said almost in unison, and Clay took in the looks of horror on their faces.

'Well, not funny, of course, not really, but in the circumstances ... well, at the time it seemed funny, this guy all shot up and his leg bleeding like mad and the sergeant pushing him and he's shouting, 'I'm fine! I'm fine! Tell 'em I'm fine! He wasn't fine at all really, but he will be.' Clay attempted an encouraging note. 'That field hospital was real good at what they do, no doubt about that, he was in good hands, so I'm sure he'll be fine.' He looked at them anxiously. 'Anyway, he really was thinking of you folks, and so when I got here I thought I'd just phone....'

'And we are really grateful you did,' Anna said. 'When you have no news at all even a tiny bit is welcome.'

'What was this field hospital called?' Victoria said. 'At least I could write there.'

'Trouble is they move,' Clay said. 'They're probably somewhere else by now and he will have been moved to a proper hospital. But I can tell you where to send to the main Medical headquarters there, they'll probably trace him.'

'Thank you,' she said, miserably.

Clay wrote out the address on paper Anna found from a drawer, and then Clancy said, 'We should love you to stay longer, Clay, but if you're going to catch your train we had better leave.'

'Yes, thanks so much.' In the hall, Clay turned. 'It's been great meeting you folks, and thanks for the lovely dinner. I haven't had nosh like that since … well, since never, to be honest.'

'We've enjoyed meeting you, Clay,' Anna said. 'If you're ever this way again, come and see us.'

'Gosh, Mrs. Sullivan, I'll never be this way again. If I get home to Wisconsin I'm never gonna leave.'

They waved the car away, and then Victoria and Anna went back to the dining room and began to clear the plates.

'Well, we haven't found out much,' Anna said. 'Only that he's wounded.' She looked at Victoria's closed face. 'Try not to worry dear.'

Victoria turned away. He had a badly shot up leg, perhaps he had bled to death. She could hear Major Simons talking to her about sepsis, and how many men died because their wounds weren't cleaned and dressed quickly enough. Perhaps that was why he hadn't written after all….

Anna's voice broke in. 'Vicki, are you OK?' Her smile was concerned. 'Don't worry,' she repeated.

Victoria made an effort. 'I'll try,' she said. 'In any case, we've got something else to worry about. Chiara's letter.'

'Oh yes, is the baby alright?'

'The baby is fine,' Victoria said. 'And guess what? He or she has a new father. Chiara and Giorgio were married a few weeks ago.'

CHAPTER TWENTY-FOUR

Victoria read and re-read the letter, trying to understand. She found it difficult to deal with the profound sense of shock she had felt at the news of the marriage. It was only a few months since Chiara had said she knew Giorgio was in love with her, Victoria. What had happened? It was a letter written with obvious care, in the excellent English typical of Chiara, and Victoria sensed the bravery that Chiara had always displayed and which she could not help but admire. She read it again:

My dear Victoria,

I am writing to let you know that after a lot of heart searching, I have decided that my baby has to be my first priority now, and for this reason Giorgio and I were married a few days ago. It was a quiet ceremony with just a few friends present. I am sure that at first you will think this to be a strange decision and you may be disappointed in me, and so I feel we owe you an explanation.

I think you know how much James and I loved each other, his death was the worst thing that has ever happened to me, and I want you to know that we had discussed a future together after the war. What we had was not one of those temporary liaisons that happen in wartime, we had made commitments to each other and I know James was looking forward to a life together, as I was.

Now, that can never be, but I know James would be so glad I am carrying his child, and above all would want a good future for him or her, and that future must be with myself, as his chosen partner. I know that Italy can recover from this awful time, and I want my baby to grow up here among friends, who will love and support me and my child.

Life is very hard for an unmarried mother here, and so the best chance of a good fulfilling life for my child was certainly for me to be married, preferably quickly. Giorgio talked to me about this, and even put forward a few names of suitable partners for me. I know you will say he was interfering but he really was trying to do his best for me. It was only when I saw his complete devotion to making me safe and the child provided for, that I realized I could never have a better husband than him. I know him very well, he is responsible and has a good income from his various businesses, he's not bad looking and he keeps his word. I thought about it for a while and then I asked him why he didn't marry me himself. He seemed quite shocked at first! That was when I told him I knew that he was in love with you. He did not deny it, but he said he knew it could never be, as your backgrounds were so different it would never work. He said he thought you were in love with Guy, and if you were that would be right for you and you could be happy.

He thought about it for a couple days and then he turned up with a huge diamond ring and asked me formally to marry him. As I have no parents alive he had been to see Julio to ask his permission! I think it's the first time he has asked permission from anyone for anything!

I know you will be concerned about what you call the Mafia connection. I do not think of it in the same way as you do. Giorgio is now the senior member of his family since his grandfather passed away and it will be largely up to him how things proceed in the future. I cannot interfere in this and wouldn't want to. I will trust our future to Giorgio and I hope you understand this. From one point of view, you might assume we have both settled for something that may be less than we hoped for, but from which we can make a comfortable and happy life together.

Guiditta sends her best love, needless to say she is delighted!
Your loving friend,
Chiara.

No matter how much she thought about it, the questions would not go away. If she thought of Giorgio in purely personal terms, Victoria had to admit he had only ever shown her kindness and consideration. Yet he often acted arrogantly, going ahead with his plans as if he always knew best. She had to admit he was often right – well, always, if you came down to it. But this was surely because he knew the territory and how everything worked, it didn't give him God-given rights to decide every bloody thing….

What on earth would Dada say? To have his only grandchild taken over by a Mafia boss, one of the family that had almost ruined his business and his marriage? Yes, it had been long ago, but that didn't make it any easier.

Was it even anything to do with her family? According to Giorgio's philosophy, it was. The child was, of course, a "blood relative" of her family and herself. Could it be that Giorgio wanted the child to replace the one which he believed had been taken from his family … Victoria herself? Or was that a mean assumption, born of her own prejudice?

Anna's reaction to the letter was a little more generous than Victoria's. As they sat together in the lounge the following evening, she confided that she thought Chiara sounded a truly fine person, one who was trying to make the best of a terrible situation. 'I was in that situation myself once,' she said. 'I know how frightening it can be.'

'But Mom, she had other choices,' Victoria said. 'She knew she could come here, I told her that before I left. She could have had a place with James's family if she wanted it.'

'But she didn't want it, and that's the point. It might have been good for us, we should have loved to have Chiara and the little one here. But what about Chiara? To be torn from her own society and plunged into a world she didn't know, and with a new baby –'

'But –'

'Anyway,' Anna said firmly, 'it was not our decision, it was Chiara's. You really can't go around dictating what everyone else ought to do, you know.'

Good heavens! That's what I think Giorgio's always doing. Am I like Giorgio? Aloud, she said, 'What do you suppose Dada will say?' Clancy was away on a business trip for a few days, having left the morning after Clay Summersbee's visit, and they had decided not to show him the letter until his return.

'He won't be too pleased, I shouldn't think,' said Anna. She considered. 'He'll be pleased Chiara has married, perhaps, to give the child a father, but he won't be pleased about the choice. Then again, it's not his decision. People have to make their own way in life.' She rose. 'Would you like a cup of tea? I think I'll have one. At home we always had a cup of tea if there was a family crisis.'

'Please.' Victoria smiled. She loved the way her mother served tea, in the English way. It did seem to help, although not when it was made in the one of the various disgusting ways that Americans thought constituted a cup of tea. When it came she got up to take the tray as her mother said, 'Is it Guy, dear? I sense a great deal of worry about you since Clay Summersbee came. I haven't wanted to pry but I wondered ... it isn't just about Chiara and Giorgio, is it?'

'No,' Victoria admitted. She stirred the teapot and left it to brew. 'Mom, I only knew him a short time in Italy, but somehow, well we....' She faltered.

'Were you lovers?' Anna asked gently.

'Good heavens, no!' Victoria was shocked at her mother's directness. 'We were ... we just seemed to like each other, he was fun, and I really liked him ... I do like him....

'Are you in love with him?'

'I ... I think I might be.' It seemed odd to be talking about it, especially to her Mom.

She got up again and started to pour the tea. 'I mean ... how do you know? I only know I can't stop thinking about him, worrying if he is OK, worrying about him worrying.... Chiara thought he felt guilty about James, because he survived and James didn't.'

'Chiara sounds to me a very sensitive girl.' Anna took her cup and saucer. 'You know what you might enjoy,' she said, changing the subject, 'a trip to see Lottie. She's old now but she still has all her marbles.'

'Oh, I would love to see her again.' Victoria adored her old nanny, who had helped bring up her and James. 'Is she well?'

'Pretty good for her age, but of course, very cut up about James. I went to tell her the news myself, and we have had a few good crying sessions together since.'

Victoria nodded. She understood why her mother suggested the visit. Lottie had been the one whose shoulder everyone cried on through the years. She had been engaged as a nanny when James was born, and had been with the family until she retired.

'I think Sunday afternoon might be good,' said Anna. 'She will be so glad to see you, she wants to hear all about Italy.'

Anna was fairly accurate about Clancy's reaction to the marriage. He was pleased the baby would have a stable background, but had some choice words to say about Giorgio.

'He's taken advantage of her situation, so he has,' he declared for the third time.

'Well, actually, I think it was her idea,' Victoria said, not believing she was defending Giorgio.

'It might help to understand her thinking if you read Chiara's letter,' Anna interceded. Clancy took it and glanced through it briefly. Then he looked up. 'Would you get me a drink please, Victoria?'

As Victoria poured his usual Scotch, he sat down and began to read the letter properly, sipping his drink and sighing occasionally. Victoria watched him taking in the contents of the letter, and thought how much she loved him, her dear, generous- minded

Dada, who would be as concerned for Chiara, someone he had never met, as if she was his daughter. He was looking tired, she decided, these business trips took it out of him and he suddenly looked his age.

At length, Clancy looked up. 'Well, I still don't like it, but I don't see that there is anything to be done. Chiara may have made a mistake but it's her life, so it is, and her decision to make.' He smiled at Victoria. 'I know you are concerned for your friend, so what we must do is support her in any way we can. We should write to her and let her know that we are always here, that she has friends and family here who will help should she ever need it.'

Victoria smiled. 'Of course you are right, Dada. I just hope everything works out well for them.'

'Perhaps we should send them a wedding present,' Clancy said. 'Think about what we could send, something –'

The front doorbell interrupted him. Victoria went to the door and came back quickly with a telegram. Her face was drained of color. She held up the telegram with a gasp. 'What if –?'

'No! No, it isn't what you think. Those have black edges....' Anna took the form and quickly opened it. 'Oh, my goodness! Oh, Clancy! Look!'

The telegram read : DELIGHTED INFORM YOUR GRANDDAUGHTER BORN TODAY STOP SIX POUNDS FOUR OUNCES STOP BOTH WELL STOP NAME JENNY CHIARA STOP CONGRATULATIONS STOP GIORGIO VETTI

Clancy fetched the champagne.

CHAPTER TWENTY-FIVE

The following Sunday afternoon, Victoria arrived at Lottie's cozy apartment at three o'clock. The old lady was delighted to see her, and their reunion was warm and happy, especially now that Victoria had such extra news to tell. Lottie had known about the impending birth, but had not realized the date might be so near. Victoria reveled in the joy brought to Lottie's face by her news.

'And her name,' she said, 'is to be Jenny Chiara.'

Lottie sat down with a bump, she seemed overcome.

'Oh, Jenny,' she said, 'dear Jenny ... she was such a darling, I was so fond of her you know, your lovely mother. Wasn't that kind of them to name her after your mother...?'

'I think it was because she was Paolo's wife,' Victoria said. 'They are looking at the baby from their family's point of view, not ours.'

'Yes, of course, but it's still the right name for her, oh, wouldn't James be proud?'

'He would have been delighted,' said Victoria, 'but we had a letter from Chiara and I've brought it for you to read....'

She sat and watched as Lottie read the letter; rather as she had watched her Dada read it days before. Lottie was undoubtedly frailer than when Victoria last saw her, and she chided herself for not having visited before now.

When Lottie finished reading she was in tears, but she raised a shining face to Victoria. 'Love is not so easily come by, you know. I'm so glad James had that, even for a short time they had that love together. Some people never find it, you know.'

'No, I suppose that's true.'

'He was such a lovely child, our little James. Always into mischief, mind … do you know he tipped the teapot into a rice pudding once? I had just made the pudding and it was cooling nicely when along came James, and oops! He was stirring it all up together with a spoon, happy as Larry! Mind, he was always kind, just a bit wild. I'm so glad there is a baby, do you think we shall ever see her?'

'Who knows? Perhaps after the war I'll be able to visit them. I still have my villa in Italy, you know, the one left to me by great uncle Vetti.'

'Hmm….' Lottie's voice was full of disdain. 'He wasn't a nice man; your Dada had his number alright. Now Paolo, your birth father, he was a lovely boy, used to come and take James out to the park and they would play football, and baseball too, they were great friends. When he married Jenny, we were all thrilled. Your mama looked lovely when she went to the wedding….'

Victoria had heard the stories many times that she switched off. She was startled back into attention by Lottie asking pointedly, 'And this Giorgio, then, what do you think of him?'

'I don't really know, Lottie. He was very good to me when the Germans came into Rome. He gave me good advice about what to do and it kept me safe. I probably would have been arrested if it hadn't been for him. As for his business activities, I know nothing about them, they seem to be proper businesses, but you never really know….'

Lottie nodded gravely, as if she was a world expert on the Mafia. But then she said, 'Well, he must have some taste if he fell for you. It isn't easy in wartime, is it? I was young in the First World War, you know. I recall the feeling, everything seems exaggerated and distorted somehow, and you can't trust your feelings….'

'Yes,' Victoria said excitedly, 'it was exactly like that. Everything so intense. You feel a moment, just a moment, of sheer beauty or … or … a lover's dream, I suppose … and then it's gone and it's dreary and the war just goes on and on….'

'But perhaps they will be alright together, Giorgio and Chiara, and of course, they have the little one to bring them together. Like you did for your Mama and Dada.'

'Did I? I didn't know that.'

'Oh yes, nothing in life is really easy, you know, not if it's worth having. And what about you, my dear? What about this friend of James's your Mama seems to think you are keen on?'

Gosh, is nothing sacred? 'Well, he's still abroad, Nana. We heard he was wounded but we don't know any more.'

'I hope you hear from him soon. Is he worth the effort, do you think? Is he the one you want?'

You bet your life on it, he's the one. You betcha! 'Yes Nana, I think he might be.'

'Well if he is, you get a move on, Vicky. You know, I think it is probably the things left undone that are those you regret in the long run…. As I said, love is not easily come by, and if there's a chance for it, make sure you're in there pitching.'

Much as she took Lottie's advice to heart, Victoria couldn't imagine how she could actually get in there and pitch. The only thing she could do was write, and she did this several times a week, both letters and V mails, using any route she could discover to try and make sure they would be delivered. It occurred to her that Guy's mother might have heard something more, and she found her address quite easily from the Army liaison unit. It was in an area of the Bronx she had never visited, and when she told Clancy she was intending to go there, he was concerned.

'I'm pretty sure that's a rough area,' he said. 'How about if I come with you?'

Victoria allowed herself a wry smile. What would he say if he knew the full extent of what she had faced in Italy?

She gave him a peck on the cheek. 'Thanks Dada.'

'I doubt if his Mom will be connected,' Victoria said as they climbed into the Buick, 'lots of older people aren't, they don't trust the phone.'

Clancy was right, it was a rundown area of mean terraced houses, most seemed to have been converted somewhat haphazardly into apartments and rooms to let. The address they had was in the middle of a block, and when they entered they were accosted by an elderly woman who demanded to know their business.

'We are looking for a Mrs. Waldman,' Clancy explained. 'I think she lives here, she has a son in the Army, we are friends of his.'

'Is he killed then?' she asked with shocking directness. She saw their look of horror and said, 'No matter if he is or not, I just thought she's been saved the knowing ... saved the bad news.'

'What do you mean?' Clancy asked.

'She's been dead these six months past. Pneumonia.'

'Oh.' Victoria wished she had thought of visiting sooner. 'Does her son know, do you think?'

'I told the Army at the time and they said they'd pass it on. I had no idea where he was, hadn't seen him for a few years, since he enlisted.' She jerked her head towards the dingy staircase leading up from the hall. 'Second floor front ... and had been here for years. She owed me a week's rent when she died, it was only because she was poorly though, she always paid her rent on time. I cleared out her things but there was only a couple bags because it was furnished. I've kept them in the storeroom for Guy. Do you want to take them now?'

'I think we'd better not,' said Clancy. 'It is Guy's business not ours, and he's sure to come home when he gets back. Do you know where she was buried?'

''Course I do! There was just enough money to bury her – well, not quite enough, but a few people in the building chipped in to make it up. They'd known her for years, you see. She had a proper funeral, quite a few folks went and I put on a little spread after, just to show respect like, 'cause she had no one, only Guy.'

She looked from one to the other, and made no objection when Clancy said, 'I'd like to pay you the week's rent that was owed, if you'll allow me, just to make matters straight for you, then I think we'll take a few flowers to the grave for Guy.'

The old woman smiled for the first time. 'That would be nice, you might tidy up a bit, I can't get down there nowadays to keep it going.' She looked out of the door to where the Buick waited. 'I'll write the address down for your chauffeur man, I don't suppose he comes down here much. When you get to the cemetery, you go in the main entrance and take the second right lane and it's about half way down.'

They stopped to buy flowers and then went directly to the cemetery, where they soon found Hannah Waldman's grave as directed. It was a poor plot but had her name inscribed on a wooden cross with R.I.P. printed underneath. Weeds had sprouted all over the small grave and Victoria immediately knelt down and started to tidy up, pulling out the weeds as the tears flowed down her cheeks. Clancy joined her, and they worked in silence until the little plot was at least tidy again.

Victoria sat back on her heels and looked at her father. 'Oh, Dada, what an awful thing. To have your Mom buried and not be able to be there. Do you think he even knows?'

'Oh yes, I should think so,' Clancy said. 'The Army are pretty good about that sort of thing. But when you think where he was and what was going on, the chances are he probably didn't know in time to do anything about it. I'm afraid this sort of thing has happened to lots of people.' He hesitated. 'You are pretty keen on this chap, aren't you? I mean Guy....'

'Yes I am, Dada,' she admitted. 'I know he came from a poor background, but he put himself through college by working at all sorts of odd jobs.'

'His mother obviously had very little,' Clancy said. 'But she had the respect of her neighbors, so she did, and had gained it in difficult circumstances. I think that is a background to be proud of, so I do.'

He smiled at her. 'Come on, little one, time to go home.'

CHAPTER TWENTY-SIX

Although the war dragged on with one day seeming very like the next, at least the news from the European front was encouraging. The Allies continued to make progress through France and into Germany, and suddenly the Boche were on the run, and rumors were rife that "it would not be long". In the Pacific region however, the fighting went on relentlessly and the news reports were sporadic and unreliable.

So it was with a feeling of disbelief that Clancy read the headline in his New York Times on May 7th 1945.

THE WAR IN EUROPE IS ENDED!
SURRENDER IS UNCONDITIONAL
V-E WILL BE PROCLAIMED TODAY
OUR TROOPS IN OKINAWA GAIN

'Anna!' he shouted, running through the house like a wild man. 'Victoria! Get down here both of you! Anna!'

It was a very happy breakfast, after they had hugged and kissed and danced around the table together. Victoria kept repeating, 'Guy is sure to be home soon,' and just as often Anna said, 'I must write to Will, they'll be over the moon in England.' But Clancy read all the details he could find, and only said, 'It's wonderful news, so it is, let's just hope the Japanese give up before too long. Then it will be really over.'

Still there was no news of Guy, until in one of her routine enquiries Victoria was told by a liaison clerk, 'Oh yes, there is a new entry here. He was discharged from hospital on the 17th April, so that means he is on his way home. He hasn't gone back to active service or that would have been recorded.' Victoria could find out nothing more.

In the meantime, at the packing factory they were busier than ever, as Anna was organizing food parcels for England. The employees of a big manufacturing company had contributed to the price of parcels to be sent to their colleagues working in their English subsidiary, and Victoria couldn't help wondering about the families who would receive them. She thought back with affection to her English family connections; her uncle Will, Anna's elder brother, and his family who still lived in the Midlands of England. She and Anna had spent a very happy holiday there just before the war, until she had heard about the bequest of the villa in Italy and had decided to go there when Anna left to return to New York. Perhaps that had been the wrong decision … if she had not done that she could have stayed with Uncle Will in England, where she would have been hungry but probably safe, as they lived in the countryside. Then James wouldn't have been ordered to go to the villa … perhaps … and she wouldn't have even met Guy … perhaps….

My English family connections, she thought ruefully. Not *blood relations* either, as Giorgio would say. But Uncle Will had said she could stay there as long as she wanted, he had called it her second home and said it might be an idea for her to stay 'until they saw what was going to happen in Italy.' Victoria sealed the last parcel for the day and reached for her jacket. It was difficult to work out just where she really belonged.

As she opened the front door, Victoria was surprised to find her Mom in the hall. 'I saw you coming,' she explained. 'I was watching for you.'

'What is it?' Her Mom seemed nervous.

'It's Guy, at long last. He telephoned.'

Victoria's heart leaped. 'Where is he? Is he here yet?'

'Yes, he's here in New York. He –'

'Is he on his way? Did you ask him to dinner?'

'No. No, I didn't. Victoria, let me explain, don't look like that.'

Anna led the way into the lounge, and said, 'It was not an easy conversation.'

'What do you mean?'

'Victoria, he's been in New York for a week.'

The blood drained from Victoria's face. *A week, he's been here a week and he hasn't been in touch until now!*

She sank slowly onto the sofa. *It obviously wasn't a priority for him, seeing me wasn't a priority....*

Anna said, 'It was rather an odd conversation, to be honest. He asked if he was speaking to Mrs Sullivan and I said 'yes', and then he said who he was, and of course I said how glad we were to hear from him, was he better? He said thank you, yes, he was quite well now, and he wondered if he could come and see us about James? I said we'd be very glad to see him and I was just going to suggest dinner tonight, and he said could he come on Thursday afternoon?'

Thursday? This is Monday!

'I said we should love to see him sooner than that if possible,' Anna continued, 'but he said he had "things to do" or something. He said if Thursday wasn't convenient he could make Friday, so I said Thursday would be fine. He's coming at three.'

'But he must have said more than that,' Victoria said. 'Did he ask about me?'

'Yes, at the end, he said, 'Will Victoria be there?' and I said 'Yes of course.' He said 'Good, that will be nice.'

Nice! What is the matter?

'Perhaps there's something wrong,' Victoria said slowly. 'Perhaps I've really put him off by sending all those letters, perhaps he thinks I'm chasing him ... did he say if he'd received them?'

'No, he didn't mention it. It wasn't an awkward conversation, he was very pleasant. It was just rather formal, that's all.'

There was really no point in discussing it, Victoria realized. There were a hundred reasons why Guy should behave a little oddly after all he had been through. The "perhaps" scenarios crowded her mind over the next few days, but nothing really made sense. Anna thought he must be very tired, and perhaps not so well, after all. He had been in hospital a long time, she told herself, knowing what Clay had said about his injury. He must also be distraught about his mother. They did not even know where he was staying, because Anna had not been given the opportunity to ask. Victoria realized she had been making assumptions about Guy which were possibly unfounded. And yet ... and yet ... she could not forget that teasing affection she had felt in Italy, that special rapport which had said something he couldn't say in words, she was sure of it. Clancy, Anna and herself all made arrangements to be there on the Thursday afternoon, and Anna made a special cake.

The inevitable day came at last, as she had always known it would. Although he would surely rather be anywhere than here, do anything rather than re-live that awful time, she knew Guy would come to see her parents. He would do it because it was the right thing to do, because it might in some small way make things easier for her parents. But to see him again? Especially after all her doubts of the last few days, could she cope with that? The mere idea of being in the same room with Guy built up such panic in her mind that she was tempted to be out when he called, but in the end she knew she would be there, for the same reason he would be there – it was the right thing to do.

When the bell rang at five minutes to, she walked calmly down the hall. Her fingers trembled as she fumbled with the latch, but she managed to open the door. She hardly recognized him, he had lost weight and was in full uniform. Their eyes met, and the panic returned with full force, so that she just smiled briefly and said, 'Oh, Guy, how nice to see you again, come on in,' and turned away, leaving him to follow her down the hall.

He caught her up quickly and reached for her arm, spinning her back to face him. He did not say anything, and after a moment she steeled herself and met his gaze. His eyes were kind, sympathetic. 'Isn't this awful?' he said.

What does that mean? Awful to meet her parents, or to face her again?

'It won't be too awful,' she said. 'My parents are looking forward to meeting you.'

'I didn't mean it that way. I meant awful that James isn't here.' His eyes clouded and she saw the misery there, perhaps he did understand, some of it anyway....

They went into the lounge and she made the introductions. When they were all seated Clancy said, 'And how is your leg now? Clay Summersbee told us it was pretty bad.'

'Who?' Guy said, then, 'Oh! Of course, I never knew his name. It was good of him to come and see you. I often wondered if he had been in touch. My leg is fine now, thanks.'

It seemed no one had anything to say, so Guy continued, 'Well, it isn't quite good as new. I have to have a few operations on it as and when it is ready.'

'Yes, you had a bad time out there,' Anna said. 'We are so glad you came to see us, Guy, we know you and James were good friends.'

His name had been mentioned and they all relaxed a little, except Guy, who was obviously ill at ease. Anna reminded him of the time when he had visited their house with the baseball team, but he only said, 'We were not in the same team, of course, James was in the college team.'

Some tea arrived but the atmosphere remained strained until Guy suddenly blurted out, 'I'm so sorry!'

'Whatever for?' Anna was genuinely bemused.

'I can't help feeling it should have been me who stayed behind, and James who should have gotten away, but there were only seconds....' He was almost in tears.

Clancy intervened. 'From what we've heard from everyone, you were given a direct order to get those files away and back to HQ. You did that, and you were right. By the way, do you think the files were important in the end? Did they help the advance?'

'I've no idea.' Guy sighed. 'But I have my doubts. The Allies were pushing on very quickly after that with the Germans in retreat towards Florence, and not wanting to stop for anything. I can't see that our information was any help at all.'

'But that's war, isn't it, son?' Clancy said. 'You have to do what is required at the time. You just obey orders and never know until ages afterwards whether or not it all made sense. You mustn't think that way, we are just glad that James had his good friend with him.'

Guy looked ready to break down, and so Victoria interrupted.

'What do you think of the news, then? I mean, about the baby?'

Guy looked at her. 'What baby?'

He had not received a single letter. Victoria could not believe it. 'But didn't you get the one I wrote when I got home?'

'I haven't received a letter at all since I left you at Alfonso's farmhouse.'

'So you don't even know about me working for the Army?'

The questions went on, but it was true. Victoria explained that she had written, over and over again, to every place she could think of, watching Guy's face change as he took in what she was saying. He shook his head in disbelief, and then said, 'When I didn't get a reply to those two letters I sent to the villa, I decided I would not send any more.' His eyes were fixed on Victoria's face. 'I thought … I thought you might have decided you didn't want to keep in touch, so I decided to wait until I got home and to contact your parents personally.'

'But I wrote every week, twice a week,' Victoria cried. 'Wait a moment ... wait....'

She dashed out of the room, returning with her purse, and a few moments later she extracted a crumpled piece of paper. 'There,' she said. 'That's the note you gave me with your details ... you gave it to me just before you left. That's the information I have been using.'

Guy took the paper and then buried his head in his hands. 'There's a mistake,' he said. 'My army number has two digits the wrong way round ... no wonder nothing got to me.'

'But surely, when I kept enquiring ... surely they could have traced you through your name...?'

'Have you any idea the amount of mail that has been going back and forth?' Guy said, smiling. 'Planeloads of it, thousands of tons every week. That's why they brought out the V mail system, the mail was filling planes needed for equipment and supplies. It's my fault, I wrote down the wrong number ... I'll bet when I enquire and give them this number, they'll trace them fast enough.'

'I seem to recall we were all in a bit of a state on that morning,' Victoria said. 'But this means you still don't know all the other news since then ... as well as the baby.'

'Like what?'

'Like Giorgio and Chiara getting married ... and the baby being a girl and being called Jenny Chiara....'

CHAPTER TWENTY SEVEN

17th June 1946

It was only seven o'clock, and she didn't need to get up until eight at the earliest. This had been decreed by her mother the previous evening, when she insisted on Victoria having an early night. She snuggled down into the warmth and comfort of her big bed and tried to relax back into blissful sleep....

The images of the past year insisted upon playing their little games behind her closed eyelids, imposing themselves into her dozing reverie, gentle reminders of the way her life had changed, each day bringing its own small message of joy or sadness, acceptance or revelation.

She thought back to the afternoon a year ago, when Guy had first come to the house, uncertain about his welcome and his future. She smiled when she recalled how he had not come to see her for a week after that; he had chased up a huge backlog of her letters and wanted to read them, in date order, so he could feel himself catching up, to some extent at least. After that …. She almost laughed out loud to think of her plans at that time. She wanted to get to know Guy properly, she recalled, and had had some ideas about gentle walks in the park and quiet dinners together, getting to know each other slowly and simply, without the stresses and strains that had always been present. She winced, remembering how quickly her plans had been shattered. She had invited him for supper, and as soon as he arrived, she said, 'There's no one in. Mom has gone to a meeting and Dada won't be home until late.'

He smiled. 'And so?'

'And so we have the house to ourselves. Would you like a drink? Supper's almost ready.'

'That would be nice.'

'Wine? Or Scotch?'

'Wine, please.'

Victoria filled a glass and brought it over. Their fingers touched slightly as he took it, and she felt a shock run through her body. She filled her own glass and sat beside him on the sofa. She sipped her wine and could feel him watching her.

'Supper's almost ready,' she said, but as she met his eyes, she knew they wouldn't be eating any time soon.

'Afterwards,' he said, picking up his glass and taking her hand. 'Bring the bottle.' He led her upstairs, where he stopped, disconcerted.

'This way,' she laughed, leading the way to her bedroom. Once there they collapsed on the bed together, and Victoria couldn't help but see the sharp grimace which crossed his face.

'It's OK,' he said. 'It's just my leg…,'

'Let me see,' she said gently.

At first he demurred, but as Victoria began to unbutton his pants, he said, 'Are you sure you want to see this? It's not pretty.'

'Of course. I want to know everything about you,' and she helped pull the pants down.

Even in the failing evening light it was appalling. Scars covered his leg from mid thigh to just above the ankle, and although some smaller ones had faded to silvery tracks, the worst were thick wedges, cutting across the smooth muscles. The lines of his bone and muscle were still graceful and strong, but within the scars the flesh had twisted and healed into deep fissures. Victoria could not bear to imagine the moment when this had been done, and how it had happened. She bent her lips to the scars and kissed the length of his leg, until Guy lifted her face to him, and said, 'I have another leg too, a good one.'

'Yes, I know, but this one needs special attention.'

'Good heavens! My mother warned me about women like you....' He pulled her down on top of him and kissed her soundly. When they parted, he began to unbutton her blouse and said, 'This is my job, you know, I've been waiting long enough.' In moments he was on top and exploring her breasts with long, gentle fingers.

'You know all about it, do you?' she countered, closing her eyes and savoring every moment. 'Nobody loves a smart-ass, you know....'

'He kissed her again. 'I think you do,' he whispered.

'Yes, I do.'

After that they could never get enough of each other, and were swept away by the need to be near, to make love again and again, to repair the damage caused by being apart for so long. And on this, the morning of her wedding, Victoria smiled and snuggled down into the warmth indulgently, forgiving herself for behaving like a wanton.

They had, of course, gotten to know each other in other ways too, there had been the quiet walks and the intimate dinners, the long conversations after sex, and she understood now how deep were the reservations Guy had felt about their ever being together. It had taken her quite a time to realize that Guy had always thought she was too good for him: something to do with his upbringing and his awful father. When she pointed out that her own father was a Mafioso, Guy took quite a while to come to terms with this new idea, having always thought of Clancy Sullivan as her father.

'Giorgio wouldn't agree with you,' she had said. 'All that stuff about blood relatives ... it must be strange for him to be bringing up a child that isn't his own. I wonder if he still thinks in the same way now?'

It was an intriguing thought, but why was she half dreaming about Giorgio? On this day of all days? A tap on the door interrupted her thoughts and her Mom came in with a steaming mug of tea.

'I thought you might be awake,' she said, as Victoria emerged from the bedclothes. 'I'll go and get you some breakfast in a moment. You can choose whatever you like today!'

Victoria smiled. 'I'd better not have too much,' she said. 'I don't want to spoil the wedding breakfast.'

'No.' Her mother smiled. She had been in charge of the food, as always, and Victoria knew it would be very special.

'Is Dada up yet?'

'Yes, he's gone out already.'

'This early? Where has he gone? He's not going into work on my wedding day?'

'No, of course not. He's off on some mission he won't tell me about, I think it might be a surprise, you know what he's like.'

Victoria said seriously, 'You know, Mom, I'll never be able to thank him enough – well, both of you, for what you have done for Guy. He was absolutely adrift a year ago, and now he knows where he's going. Dada has been great....'

'Well, he was going to take on some senior managers from the Government G I scheme, Guy might as well be one of them. And Dada really likes him, and he works hard … you know, your Dada would never "make" him a job, Guy's had to prove his worth.'

'He'll do that OK, I never knew anyone so anxious to make his own way. It's all about male pride, isn't it? Was Dada like that when he was young?'

Her mother sat down on the edge of the bed. 'Times were different then,' she said softly. 'It wasn't a matter of pride or anything else. It was just about survival. When we first came here, all we could do was try to make enough to pay our way until the end of the week. It was a matter of working hard, and if you saw an opening of any sort, you just went after it, no questions asked.'

She smiled, and then admitted, 'Our first real chance was down to your Dada. He was working in a factory and the catering manager was sacked, for both incompetence and fiddling the books. Your Dada went to see the boss and told him that his wife was a wonderful cook who could do the job ten times better for half the cost. It was amazing they listened to him, but they gave me a chance and everything grew from there.' She laughed. 'If it had been left to me, we should still be working for someone else. I never had the confidence to take a risk, but your Dada could always see what was needed.'

She rose and went to the window. 'It's going to be a lovely day, sunny but a little breeze I think, the perfect wedding day. Now, what would you like for breakfast?'

'Where is he?' Victoria fussed. 'I shall have to go and get dressed soon. I don't want him being late taking me to the church. I don't expect he's dressed for church, either.' The doorbell rang. 'Ah! At last ... there he is.'

Anna was on her way. 'No, he'd have his key, surely?'

She opened the door and turned to Victoria. 'It's the flowers, dear, come and look. They are so beautiful.'

They were indeed beautiful. Victoria's bouquet was of long-stemmed red roses and lily-of-the-valley, a suggestion of her Mom's to remind her of the roses that Victoria's father Paolo had always sent to Anna on her birthday.

There was another, smaller bouquet too, of mixed fragrant freesias, together with corsages for Anna and Lottie, and buttonholes for the men.

'Who is this for?' Victoria picked up the freesias. 'They've sent extra ... there's an extra corsage as well, and too many buttonholes ... they must have gotten our order mixed up with someone else's.'

Before Anna could answer, the door opened and Clancy came in, looking a little disheveled.

'Thank goodness!' Anna said, but Clancy only laughed and said, 'I have a surprise for you, little one. We have a few extra guests for the wedding.'

He opened the door and suddenly, inexplicably, Giorgio was in the hallway, almost filling it with his big presence and smile, and behind him came Chiara, her beautiful face wreathed in smiles. They embraced Victoria thoroughly, all talking and laughing at once, explaining they had arrived the day before and had been staying in town. Clancy had picked them up. 'You didn't think we would miss your wedding, did you, cousin?' Giorgio asked.

'But didn't you bring Jenny?' Even as Victoria said it the door opened again and in came Guiditta, holding the little one in her arms. Victoria was overcome to see her old friend, in her wildest dreams she could never have imagined that Guiditta would dare to get on a plane, never mind visit America. As the tears coursed down her cheeks, she knew that this would be the day the healing really began.

As they all crowded into the lounge, she could not believe they were all there, the friends who had shared her trials, the people she trusted and loved. She gazed at Guiditta, cooing at the baby with Anna, and asked Chiara, 'How on earth did you persuade Guiditta to come?'

'I couldn't,' Chiara said. 'But Giorgio managed it.'

Victoria and Guy spent the last day of their honeymoon walking in the mountains near their holiday retreat, a small log cabin in the Adirondacks. The "Italian branch of the family" as Clancy called them, should be back in Rome already, with Guiditta happily planning further refurbishment of the villa.

Victoria turned to Guy, and he saw her slight frown.

'There's something I have to tell you,' she said, hesitantly.

'I've guessed it,' Guy said. 'You've decided the whole thing was a big mistake and you want to go back to Italy....'

'You wish! You don't get rid of me so easily. In fact, you have even more responsibilities than you realize.' She took a deep breath and announced, 'I'm going to have a baby.'

That shut him up for a moment only, and then he said, 'What?' He stared at her. Then, ' Wow!' he yelled. He was actually jumping up and down with excitement, but stopped quickly as his leg hurt.

Victoria glanced around to see if they were observed, but they were alone.

'What an old softie you are,' she said, taking his arm. 'I wasn't sure you would be pleased.'

'What? Of course I'm pleased, it must be the best thing to happen to me since ... since we got married.' He laughed. 'How long have you known?'

'I knew just before we got married,' she told him. 'But I wanted to keep it to myself for a while.'

Guy took her in his arms. 'It's wonderful news, darling. Have you seen a doctor?'

'Yes, and it's confirmed and all is fine, so don't start fussing.'

'I won't.'

They walked on arm in arm. Then Guy said urgently, 'My God! Where are we going to live?'

'With Mom and Dada, at first, just as we arranged.'

'But not now, surely, with a baby on the way?'

'It isn't a problem. And you know it isn't. They will help us, that is, if you can come down off your high horse and accept it.'

'Out of the question,' Guy responded. 'Clancy has done far too much for me already, and I'm going to work like hell to pay him back. I want to earn my own living, not scrounge from your dad.'

'I know, I know. But we've no real problems, have we? Apart from your leg, I mean?'

Guy smiled. The doctor had promised there would be a vast improvement after another four or possibly five operations on his leg, to be carried out over the next few years. 'Not really, but I'm not much of a catch, am I?' he said. 'No money and a gammy leg, and a job only because of your dad's kindness, and an immediate future of operations and time off work, and no real experience and nowhere to live and a baby on the way, but it could be worse....' He stopped. Victoria was laughing.

'I'm sorry,' she said. 'It just reminded me of that guy who came to see us, that soldier, Clay from Wisconsin. He said you were in an awful state, bleeding and being pushed around, and you kept saying, 'I'm fine! Tell them I'm fine!'

She linked her arm into his. She knew what Clay meant now, and she knew they would be fine. They paused for a moment under a huge elm, and Guy drew her into his arms. 'And you my love?' he said. 'All that stuff about wondering who you were and where you belonged? Are you clear now?'

She nodded and looked up at him.

'I belong with you.'

He lowered his head and kissed her, long and slow.

AUTHOR'S NOTE.

The Ardeatine Cave Massacre, as it came to be called, was the worst war crime to occur during the Second World War in Rome. After the city was liberated the arduous work of recovering and identifying the bodies was undertaken by a team headed by Dr Atillio Ascarelli, and due to their painstaking efforts 324 of the 335 victims were eventually identified. Dr Ascarelli was later posthumously decorated by the President of Italy with the *Medaglia d'Argento* for his work.

On March 24th 1949 the Ardeatine caves were consecrated as a national monument. The area is marked by a sculpture in marble by Francesco Coccia, and a mausoleum inside the caves holds 335 sarcophagi, which contain the remains of the victims.

Twenty years after the massacre, an American journalist Robert Katz wrote a book called 'Death in Rome' which attempted to discover the truth about those dreadful events. In 1963 a powerful anti-war film was based on the book. Titled *Massacre in Rome,* it starred Richard Burton and Marcello Mastroianni, and was directed by Carlo Ponti .

OTHER BOOKS BY HELEN SPRING.

If you have enjoyed this book, you may like to read Helen Spring's other works:

The Chainmakers. (The prequel to Blood Relatives.)

Strands of Gold

Memories of the Curlew

All are available on Amazon or any good bookshop, or www.FeedARead.co.uk. They are also available as e-books from Amazon Kindle, or from www.helenspring.co.uk where you can find out more and read excerpts from the books.